PRAISE FOR *Columbo: The Helter Skelter Murders*

"We know who, what, when, how, and why from the start. The fun is watching Columbo—polite, oblique, and seemingly distracted—disassemble the 'perfect' crime while playing cat and mouse with his suspects. If readers like the TV

The New York Daily News

"A smart, fast, and completely captivating novel for every taste."
                                                    —*Mystery Scene*

"Readers who are not familiar with the TV show will be delighted to get a very entertaining mystery, a new angle on the assassination attempt, and an introduction to a hero who is as delightful on the page as he must be on television."
                                                    —*Rapport*

COLUMBO:
THE GAME SHOW KILLER

WILLIAM HARRINGTON

A TOM DOHERTY ASSOCIATES BOOK
NEW YORK

This is a work of fiction. All the characters and events portrayed in this book are either products of the author's imagination or are used fictitiously.

COLUMBO: THE GAME SHOW KILLER

Copyright © 1996 by MCA Publishing Rights, a Division of MCA, Inc.

Cover art by Dan Gonzalez

A Forge Book
Published by Tom Doherty Associates, Inc.
175 Fifth Avenue
New York, NY 10010

Forge® is a registered trademark of Tom Doherty Associates, Inc.

ISBN: 0-812-55080-3
Library of Congress Card Catalog Number: 95-53097

First edition: August 1996
First mass market edition: July 1997

Printed in the United States of America

0 9 8 7 6 5 4 3 2 1

Note to Reader

This is a work of fiction. All the characters
and events portrayed in this novel are
fictitious or are used fictitiously.

I affectionately dedicate this book to my sister Jane, her husband, Tom, and their children and grandchildren.

"Well, Sir, we do like to find
out who kills people and why."

ONE

Tuesday, April 4—7:58 P.M.

The stools in the dimly lit bar of the Pacific Club were upholstered in tan leather. They had arms and thickly padded seats. When Grant Kellogg lifted himself onto one of them just before eight o'clock he was emotionally drained and physically exhausted. He was acutely conscious of his fatigue. He told himself he could not remember a time when he had been so tired.

"Congratulations, Mr. Kellogg."

Emily, the petite topless barmaid, put in front of him a Beefeater martini on the rocks with a twist. She didn't have to be told that was what he wanted.

The sight of the girl was enough to lift a man's spirits. She was delicately, youthfully beautiful, with dark-brown hair neatly brushed back, and with an innocent, open face dominated by wide blue eyes. It was a strict rule of the club that a girl who worked there would be fired if she accepted any sort of proposition from a member—and that he would lose his membership. It had happened. It was the only reason he did not offer her a thousand dollars. Well . . . five hundred.

"There's been nothing but you on television all evening," she said.

He nodded. "Price and I," he sighed.

"I knew he wasn't guilty. I just knew he wasn't. And when he got *you* to defend him— Well, the poor DA never had a chance, did he?"

"I wouldn't say that, Emily. I was never sure we'd get Price off. When that jury came back—" He shook his head. "You can't imagine the tension."

"I can imagine. I was watching. And, hey, when I said to some friends of mine that I'd probably be serving drinks to Grant Kellogg tonight— Hey! Anyway, congratulations, Mr. Kellogg."

"Thank you. You're very kind—besides being a lovely girl."

It was said that Grant Kellogg's appearance, presence, and manner were major elements of his success as a trial lawyer. He was a big man with broad shoulders. His hair had turned white before he was thirty-five, but it had never thinned. His complexion was ruddy—the result maybe of his consumption of thousands of bottles of Beefeater gin. His eyes, peering out from narrow slits, were pale blue and focused in a hypnotic stare. He wore perfectly tailored suits with white shirts and striped ties. He favored French cuffs and heavy gold cuff links.

Lawyers who thought his success was dependent on his rhetorical flamboyance in the courtroom were the lawyers he most often overpowered. The truth was that Grant Kellogg was a hardworking lawyer who came into the courtroom thoroughly *prepared* to try his cases. He came prepared with meticulously researched law and with total mastery of the facts. Besides having an almost-photographic memory, he came to court with a laptop computer, which one of his associates used to check law and facts as the trial progressed.

Jim Price was a film producer, a handsome man, a notorious womanizer, a gossip-column-and-tabloid celebrity, and a Hollywood iconoclast. More than a few in the community had been amused and pleased when he was charged with the murder of his wife. The whole nation had been obsessively fascinated with every detail of his case. Acquitted at four this afternoon, he would be in bed with Bonnie by now, laboring to make up for eleven months in jail. He had signed a contract to produce a book about his experience. It would be a tissue of lies. It had better be. Whatever he wrote—or had written for him—he'd make a fortune from it.

Emily had served a man and woman down the bar, and now she returned. "If I ever get accused of anything. . . ," she said with a wide smile.

"Don't ever get accused of anything, Emily. But if you do, I'll defend you."

"I couldn't afford you, Mr. Kellogg."

"Gratis."

"Would you, really?"

"Of course."

"Another martini?"

He nodded. He hadn't finished the first one, but he knew he'd want another. And maybe a third. Then he'd go downstairs for dinner.

"Hello, Grant!"

Now he knew he'd want a third drink. If there was anyone he didn't need to see, it was Chalmers Willoughby.

"Congratulations, Grant. Another brilliant performance."

"Thank you. Pull up a stool." There was no point in not welcoming Chalmers; he was going to sit down anyway. "I think I lost ten pounds trying that case. Do my clothes look funny?"

"*Your* clothes *never* look funny. You always have about you that certain *je ne sais quoi*. Style, I guess it's called."

"I try."

"Black Label, Mr. Willoughby?"

Willoughby nodded at Emily. "On the rocks. You're looking beautiful, as usual."

"Thank you."

No matter if he tried or didn't, and no matter how hard he tried, Chalmers Willoughby could not appeal to a girl like Emily or put her at ease. In her case, he stared too hard. With other women, he spoke with too much intense sincerity and said clumsy things. He was dull. He had no élan. Fifty years old, with thinning black hair but big bushy eyebrows, he was not an unattractive man, but his want of grace put him in distinct contrast to Grant Kellogg.

Emily put his drink in front of Willoughby, then moved down the bar to allow the two men to talk privately. Willoughby watched her. His appraising eyes chilled her.

"I suppose she wants to get into show business," he said to Grant.

"Don't they all? I'd say she's *already* in show business."

"Yes. She surely is. Well . . . congratulations again."

Willoughby stared at his drink for a moment, then stared at Emily again, and finally looked at Grant. "I don't suppose this is the best time or place to mention it, but sometime we're going to have to talk about your notes."

"I have no doubt," Grant said dryly.

"I think you'll agree that the bank has not been demanding."

"No. The bank has been very fair."

"You must have gotten a tremendous fee from Price."

"Do you want to know? You're my banker; you're entitled to know. He has paid me a million dollars."

"My god, then—"

Grant nodded. " 'My god' is right. I'd be glad to have you go through my books and see where that money went. To start with, I paid Duke $4,000 a day to sit with me as co-counsel at trial—also to spend his evenings with me, going over the testimony and all the rulings, which is not an unreasonable amount for a lawyer who can make $400 an hour with no trouble. And he was worth it. We were in trial for fifty-eight days, which cost me $232,000. Besides that, he billed me for eight days of trial preparation—another $32,000. Lila, my young associate, gets $85,000 a year, and her time was wholly devoted to the case for eight months. There's $56,000. I had to hire a law student to do research and write memoranda of law for me. She cost me $12,000. I had the court reporter delivering tapes to us at the end of every day of trial, which tapes we put in computer memory so we could review testimony. For fifty-eight days, that process cost me something like $40,000. LEXIS and NEXIS computer research is invaluable, but not cheap. I paid artists to make charts, messengers to run documents back and forth, and so on. I had more than $382,000 in expenses."

"Grant—"

"I had to guarantee the fees and travel expenses of the expert witnesses, eleven of them. Price is supposed to pay those fees and expenses, but he hasn't been able to so far, so I'm out more than $150,000 that I may or may not get from him. Besides that, he is supposed to pay for the jury-research outfit we used. That's $30,000 more that I won't get until he gets his book out."

"Grant—"

"To keep my office, just to have my office: building space, secretaries, phones, equipment, insurance, and all the rest— Say, $28,000 a month, minimum. I had the Price case for eleven months, and it averages out that eight months were exclusively devoted to his defense. That makes $224,000 office costs."

"Grant—"

"Attributable to the Price defense: about $786,000. The million doesn't look like so much now, does it?"

"Grant—"

"I gave eight months of my professional time to the case. So I've got, say, a little more than $214,000 left for eight months of my professional life. Out of which I've got to pay income taxes. So I'm a fuckin' millionaire?"

Emily detected a break in the conversation and approached to ask if either man wanted another drink. Both agreed to another round.

Willoughby shook his head. "What you're telling me is that Price paid you a million dollars to defend him, which is going to leave you not very well fixed, but he's going to sell his story for so much that *he'll* wind up *very* well fixed."

Grant tossed back the last of his second martini. "You've got it. He killed his wife and—"

"Grant!"

"He did. We may as well say it. He's been acquitted and can't be tried again. He killed his wife, and he's going to make more money from the story than he could have made producing films during the months he was in jail. I mean, god almighty, nothing sells better than an accused and acquitted celebrity. Besides the book he's gonna do, he'll be appearing on television—not just tabloid TV, but on supposedly respectable news shows—and . . . Christ! I sometimes think I should kill somebody myself. There's no better way to make really big money. Of course, I'm not a celebrity in the way Price is. Damn it!"

"Why don't *you* write a book on the Price trial?"

"I'd like to, but Price and his publisher and ghostwriter went to work on it five months ago. You know what? I was approached. But, damn it, Chalmers, you can't prepare and try a case and write a book about it at the same time! Do you have any idea how many witnesses and potential witnesses I had to interview? How many motions I had to prepare and argue? How many preliminary hearings I had to attend? Christ, man! I put in twelve- and fourteen-hour days on the Price defense, *before* we went to trial—sixteen-hour days when we *were* in trial. Even if I'd had a ghost, I didn't have time to put my thoughts together and give the guy something to work on."

"I think I understand."

"I think you do. Most people think handling big criminal cases is glamorous and lucrative." Grant paused and sighed noisily. "Try it, my friend." He shook his head. "It's a trap. I wish I could get out of it and work on accident cases, property cases, and so on. I can't. Before the week is over, somebody with more money than good sense will commit some awful crime and offer me what looks like big money to defend."

Chalmers Willoughby sipped Scotch and nodded sympathetically. "I will welcome the opportunity to do anything I can to help you, Grant. But . . . We *must* sometime begin working out a payment plan to retire your notes."

"I am well aware of that."

2

He knew his limit. A fourth martini was all right. A fifth would be one too many. Chalmers Willoughby left, and Emily came over to chat.

"I'd like to become a lawyer," she said. "I'd really like that."

"Why don't you?"

She smiled wistfully. "Well, I'm twenty-three, and I've only got two years of college. Y' know, I go to USC. I'd have to finish my degree and then go to law school." She shook her head. "I don't think I could afford it."

"You must make pretty good money here."

She nodded. "That's why I do it. Even so, I don't think I could afford law school. I'd have to quit this job."

"Why?"

"Well . . . Wouldn't I?"

"I don't see why. You can go to school in the daytime and work here at night."

"Would you take me into your office as an associate?"

He grinned. "You get admitted to the California Bar, you've got a job."

Emily laughed happily. "Oh," she said. "Here's Miss Björling. Your usual, Miss Björling?"

Erika Björling climbed onto the bar stool beside Grant. She was a stunning woman who captured the attention of any room she entered. Everyone recognized her. For nineteen years she had appeared on prime-time television every evening as second banana of the game show *Try It Once.* Hired originally as a model to pull curtains and show off prizes, she had graduated to a more important role: the game show squealer. Her chief function had been to generate enthusiasm by jumping up and down and squealing in mock delight when a contestant won a prize. Also, she had been straight woman to the host, though occasionally the writers fed her a comic line or two. She had exactly what her role required: a spectacular figure and the blandly gorgeous face of the stereotypical California blond. These assets had not sold well since *Try It Once* was canceled two years ago, and she was unemployed and unhappy.

"Congratulations," she said to Grant. "Another triumph."

"Right. Another triumph. For all it's worth."

He could speak to Erika with complete candor. A good many years ago, they had been lovers for a few months, and they had been friends ever since. The tabloids had given their affair only a little attention: a paragraph or two on inside pages. She had been a conspicuous celebrity. He had not been—not then—and a liaison between the glamorous game show squealer and a coming young lawyer was no big scandal. Tabloid rumors had linked her to such figures as Cary Grant and William Holden. These rumors, unsubstantiated by any facts their reporters ever did discover, had been sensationalized in gushing front-page headlines, while her *real* affairs were downplayed or entirely missed. The tabloids had failed to discover even a rumor of her most significant affair, with superstar Tim Wylie.

Anyway, Grant and Erika knew each other's secrets and concealed nothing much from each other.

"Don't play world-weary cynic, Grant. You know you *glory* in the acquittal you just won. You also know the son of a bitch would likely be on his way to San Quentin if not for you."

Emily put his fourth martini in front of Grant and a double shot of Jack Daniel's Black Label in front of Erika.

"I missed your show," he said.

"Don't make sick jokes. I don't want you to watch me—don't want *anybody* to watch me—sitting there with other has-beens, trying to solve dumb riddles. I don't want to know the kind of people who watch celebrity panel shows."

"You didn't want to know the kind of people who watched *Try It Once*."

"I'm going to do another dinner-theater play next month. I wouldn't mind if you came to see me in that. It will run all of two weeks, so you'll have to amend your schedule to make it."

He knew the story. Since *Try It Once* was cancelled, Erika had appeared a total of four times as a guest on sitcoms, had played dumb-blond roles in half a dozen dinner-theater productions, and was seen regularly only in commercials for local businesses, running only on Los Angeles stations. You could still see her now and then around LA, but in New York she was history. She was still a striking woman, but she was in her forties and had lost the novelty and freshness she had brought to the early episodes of *Try It Once*. Her gulps of Tennessee sour mash had become doubles, and she drank more of them.

"Had a couple of offers," she said.

"Yeah?"

"Uhm-hmm. One was to appear at the opening of a boutique on Rodeo Drive. All I would have had to do was walk around. They had a dress for me. Shall I call it a micromini?"

"And you said no. Good for you."

Erika nodded toward Emily. "I also had an offer to work

like that—bare-titted—at Farley's. Pretty damned good money, too."

"And you said no."

"Curtly. I haven't come to that. Maybe I will. Jesus, Grant! I made the cover of *People* magazine!"

He put his hand on hers. "You'll make it again, Erika."

She tossed back her drink. "Like hell."

TWO

Friday, April 7—8:21 P.M.

Grant and Erika met again in the club bar. She was there a few minutes before him, and Emily had poured her a double shot of Jack Daniel's Black Label. She'd drunk half of it when he arrived. She was wearing a black mini-dress trimmed with gold that did not just show her legs but displayed her chest from nipple to nipple. (One envious woman had said, "God, she'll catch pneumonia!")

"One drink here," he said. "Then to dinner. I've got something to tell you."

"I've been talking with Emily about working topless. She says you get used to it in less than half an hour."

Grant glanced at Emily. "She's young and resilient and optimistic." He put his hand on Erika's. "You aren't reduced to working bare-titted—to say it the way you put it the other night. You've got better things ahead of you than that."

Erika swallowed the rest of her whiskey and nodded to

Emily to pour her another. "You gonna find me a new job, Grant?"

"I found out something, kid. Don't get sloshed. You're going to need a clear head."

"Got something important to say to me, Grant?"

"Goddamned important."

When they walked into the dining room, the crowd fell silent for a moment. Grant Kellogg! And Erika Björling! For the moment, he was the most famous lawyer in the world. He might not be next week, but he was now. And she was— No one could say what she was, exactly, but she was a real *celebrity*.

As he had ordered, they were given one of the booths along the wall, where they could talk quietly and not be overheard. He overruled her order for another whiskey and told the waiter to bring a bottle of Châteauneuf-du-Pape.

He sat beside her and caressed her leg. "Erika . . . Get your ducks in a row. I've got something to tell you that's going to hurt. Maybe I shouldn't have asked you to dinner to hear this. Maybe we should have met in my office. I don't know. I want you to know that I care deeply for you and don't want you to—"

"Spit it out, Grant."

"I know who killed Tammy."

If he had struck her with a hammer, he could not have staggered Erika worse.

The tabloids had never discovered her affair with Tim Wylie, a Hollywood legend, the squeaky clean all-American-boy superstar. Twenty years ago, when *Try It Once* was a new show and she was being called a "starlet," she had become pregnant by Tim Wylie, whose real name was Leonard DeMoll. He was fifty years old, and she was twenty-two. She bore him a daughter she named Tammy. To preserve his image, which would have been destroyed if it had become known he was the father of an illegitimate child, Wylie had promised her he would agree to anything. She retained a young lawyer named Grant Kellogg, who dealt with Wylie's lawyers and negotiated a contractual commitment from Wylie to pay her $3,000 a month child support until Tammy was twenty-five years old—that is, until she would have graduated from college and maybe from a graduate school.

Tammy was a beautiful child, intelligent and promising in every way. But when she was fourteen she disappeared. The tabloids went into a feeding frenzy. Erika went into a clinic. Four months after Tammy disappeared, her body was found in a canyon fifty miles north of Los Angeles. The coroner identified her by her dental work. The body was so far decomposed that the medical examiner could not determine if she had been sexually abused.

That was six years ago. Erika did not return to *Try It Once* for six months, but when she did, she was greeted by a standing ovation and dozens of articles and stories about her dignity and courage. Tammy's death made Erika a far greater celebrity than she had been as a game show squealer. If she'd had talent for acting, singing, or dancing, she could have been a star, not just a celebrity.

She would gladly have worked as a topless barmaid if that would have saved Tammy.

"I'm sorry, Erika. I thought about just leaving it alone. But I think you have to know." He squeezed her hands under his. "It's worse than anything either of us could have imagined."

"What could be worse?"

"To know who did it."

"Grant . . . ?"

He sighed and took one hand off hers to wipe his eyes. "You know, not *every* client I defend gets off. I had to go up to San Quentin Wednesday to talk to a man I defended, about his appeal. He's guilty as crap. But we're appealing anyway. Not all my clients are rich and famous. Some are just felons, which is what this guy is. He told me something that— I told him I'd see to it that he spent the rest of his life up there if he was lying. He swore he wasn't. He told me who killed Tammy. And why."

Erika was crying. "Who?"

Grant drew a deep breath. "Tim . . . Leonard DeMoll."

She gasped. Then her flushed face hardened. "You believe this?"

He nodded. "My man in San Quentin told me Tim paid him $10,000 to dispose of her body. He was supposed to take it out to sea and dump it off a boat with a weight attached, so it would never be found. But he'd lied to Tim. He didn't have a boat. He just drove out and abandoned the body in the canyon."

"But *why?*"

"At the time when he murdered Tammy, Tim Wylie was in eclipse. Think about it. He's had a revival now, but at that time he hadn't made a picture in four years. He had an expensive style of life, too, you know. Also— Well, Erika, you aren't the only woman he had to pay money to. You were the only one getting monthly payments—"

"But they were for *Tammy,* not me. If I ever got $10,000 out of him that was for me, I'd be surprised. I haven't kept count."

"The payments came to $36,000 a year, and he had eleven years more to make them—$396,000 more—at a time when his income was drying up. And that's the why."

"You believe this. You're sure it's true."

"I have to believe it. Why would my man in San Quentin lie to me?"

"I'll kill the son of a bitch!"

Grant took both her hands in his and held them tightly. "Maybe you should," he said. "Maybe you just should. But let's think about it."

Her face was a mask of anger. "If I could figure a way so I wouldn't get caught—"

"Erika. Be calm. I want you to think about something. Suppose you do kill him. But suppose you do it in such a way that you and I can make five million dollars out of it. And maybe twice that."

"How? How could I do that?"

"Get caught. Go to trial, defended by me, and be acquitted. We can sell a book contract for at least a million. Probably more. We'll let the police discover that Tim Wylie was Tammy's father. That will make the story twice as delicious. We can sell interviews, TV appearances—you and I both. We might even get a pay-per-view television show—you talking about your ordeal. There can be millions in it."

"How can we be sure I'll be acquitted?"

"We'll set it up that way. We'll work it out. We won't do it until we have it set up to make acquittal absolutely certain."

"I'll have to go to jail, won't I?"

"Yes. That'll be a valuable part of the deal. Say you appear on pay-per-view. The fact that you can tearfully describe what it was like for you to be in jail will get us twice the audience. Hey! We might even be able to arrange things so you could be interviewed—say by somebody like Barbara Walters—through the bars of a cell. I mean, there's no end to—"

"How long would I have to be in jail?"

"Well . . . Jim Price was in for eleven months. But we can work faster. You'll have to figure on six months."

"For six months in the slammer I get my revenge on that bastard and a couple of million, minimum? And we can set it up so my acquittal is absolutely certain?"

"Absolutely certain."

"I don't have to do it if I feel uncertain of the acquittal?"

"You're the one who's going to do it. You can back out anytime."

Erika lifted her chin high. "Alright. Let's work on it."

MONDAY, APRIL 10—7:45 P.M.

Sonya Pavlov was working behind the bar in the Ten Strikes Lounge, adjacent to the Ten Strikes Bowling Alley. She was the manager of the lounge and not usually a bartender, but sometimes she filled in.

Grant Kellogg took a stool as far as he could get from the knot of drinkers at the end of the bar. Sonya mixed a Beefeater martini on the rocks and set it before him.

"How's it going, Sonya?"

"It's a tough damned town, Grant. You know it is." She spoke English with an accent that had diminished over the years but remained distinctly Russian.

"Oh, something may open up. I wish I could help you, but I'm afraid I have no influence where it would count."

Sonya Pavlov was thirty-five years old. She had lived in the States for about fifteen years and had been naturalized six years ago. She was a tall, husky blond. She had managed when she was in her twenties to get six brief appearances on television shows where her accent was an advantage. For most shows it was a disadvantage and limited the number of roles she could play, even though she was a striking woman and a competent actress. Tonight she wore skintight black leggings and an LA Dodgers T-shirt. The bowlers who came in the lounge would appreciate it that she was wearing no bra under the shirt and would manifest their appreciation with generous tips.

"How's the boy?"

Sonya shook her head. "Smart. I've got to get him through college some way."

"That's why I came in, to talk to you about a way to make enough money to put him through college."

"Who I have to kill?"

"Nobody. All you have to do is lie under oath."

3

9:10 P.M.

Fred Mansfield was the regular bartender in Ten Strikes. He had asked Sonya to cover for him until nine o'clock, because he had a big problem with his girlfriend and needed to take her to dinner to talk it out.

"I do you a favor, you do me," she said to him as soon as he had served three customers and had a moment.

"Sure thing, kiddo."

"How'd you like to get into a deal that can make you and me a hundred thousand bucks each?"

"Who do I gotta make dead?"

THREE

1

Erika sat on the bed in her room at King's Court Motel, nervous and impatient, watching television. She wore well-faded blue jeans and a gray sweatshirt. She had brought along two airline bottles of Jack Daniel's, to limit herself to that much, and had just tipped the second bottle and drunk a swallow when at long last the phone rang.

"Yeah?"

"King's Court."

That was all he said. It was Grant, calling from his cellular phone, and he had used the code they had agreed on that would tell her the coast was clear. Sitting across the street from the Wylie house, he had seen Faye leave the house for her usual Thursday-night bridge game. Tim was home alone.

They had thought Faye would leave an hour earlier. Erika had begun to wonder if she was going at all, if their scheme was not frustrated for this week.

Erika drank the last of the sour-mash whiskey and shoved the empty bottle into her purse. She was being careful to leave nothing in this room that could possibly identify her. In fact, she had worn white cotton gloves during the hour she had been here. She had left no fingerprints whatever.

She shoved the bottles to the bottom of the purse, leaving the pistol readily accessible without fumbling. She knew almost nothing about firearms, but Grant had given it to her and taught her how to use it. She had never actually fired it, but she had snapped it twenty times. She knew when the safety was on or off. She knew how to cock it. She knew she had eight shots.

Eight would be more than enough. The gun was a .32 caliber Colt, small enough to go in a purse, powerful enough to kill a man. But it might take two or three shots, depending on how far away she was when she fired and where she hit him.

They had rehearsed. She should step close. She should be certain to get her first shot into Wylie's chest or at least the stomach. If she missed or hit him only in the shoulder or arm, he might have enough strength to lunge and grab the gun away from her. Once he was down, she had to put a shot into his head, to be sure he died.

It was all very gruesome, but he would die more easily than Tammy had. He had *strangled* Tammy.

2

8:24 P.M.

North Perugia Way. Bel Air. Nine minutes from the motel. She did not pull her car, an MGB, British-racing-green, into the driveway where it would be visible in the lights mounted on the garage, but parked on the edge of the road. She checked the pistol one more time. Breathing heavily, she walked up the driveway to the house and rang the bell.

He answered. Tim Wylie. That was what he called himself. Actually, his name was Leonard DeMoll—hardly the name for the gangling, drawling Goody Two-Shoes he had carefully developed and maintained as a persona. He was seventy years old, and he had aged well. He had aged like such actors as Spencer Tracy and Burt Lancaster, whose graying hair and lined faces gave their later characterizations strength they had not attained when they were youthful and smooth. He was dressed as if he expected a reporter to stop by—meaning that he wore pipestem jeans, a checkered shirt, and cowboy boots. She was surprised he wasn't wearing a gunbelt and "totin' his old .44"—which he had confessed to her during pillow talk he had never fired in his life, not even blanks. He'd said he was afraid he'd blow his foot off with it—he, the man who was supposed to shoot the heads off rattlesnakes that crawled too close to his ranch house. He was a fraud. That was all he'd ever been.

"My god! Erika! Well . . . Come on in."

She stepped inside the door. He closed the door and pointed the way to the living room. She knew the way. They had conceived Tammy on the couch, while Faye was out playing bridge on Thursday evening. The television set was on, showing something noisy.

"Want a drink? I can offer bourbon. I don't keep Tennessee sour mash on hand."

"I'll have a bourbon."

He led her into the living room, where he pointed at a couch and went to a bar to pour drinks. "What are you up to?"

"Nothing. Nothing at all. I may have to take a job as a topless barmaid."

"I suppose that means you want money again. I can't go on giving you money."

Erika had needed a minute to build up her courage. Now she was ready. She rose from the couch and walked toward him.

"No, I don't want anything from you, Len. I've got something *for* you." She called him "Len," as his best friends did. "It's from Tammy."

"Well . . . " He saw the Colt automatic as she pulled it out of her purse. "Erika! *What—*"

She was calm and determined enough to point the muzzle where she wanted her bullet to go. Her first shot struck him squarely in the middle of his chest. He screamed and stumbled back. He grabbed at his chest, and blood oozed between his fingers. She stepped even closer. Her second shot went through his hands. His knees failed, and he fell on his face.

Erika held the gun in both hands and fired a shot into his ear.

As Grant had promised, the Colt had not made big explosions. Anyone hearing it might well have thought it was shooting on the television.

She returned the pistol to her purse and withdrew her white cotton gloves. She was confident no one had heard her shots, but she wanted to be out of the house as soon as possible. She knew the rooms. She ran to Len's bedroom. It was separate from Faye's. She opened a drawer in his nightstand and put a sheet of notepaper inside. The bastard kept a package of condoms there. Maybe he was expecting a visitor even tonight. She closed the drawer and returned to the living room.

There they were on the wall: *"Printemps du verger,"* by

Vincent van Gogh and signed "Vincent," *"Entrer en danse,"* by Henri de Toulouse-Lautrec, and *"Harlequins nus,"* by Pablo Picasso—each one worth three fortunes. There were five other paintings hanging in the living room, but these were the three Grant had said she should take. She went to the van Gogh and pulled it from the wall. It did not come away easily, and she wondered if jerking it off the wall had not activated an alarm. She listened and didn't hear anything, but—

Here was a fault in their plan. Taking the three paintings would create a motive for the murder. But, she realized now, she had already risked setting off an alarm, and she realized further that she could not carry all three to her car at once. She'd have to take the van Gogh out first—or maybe two of them—and return for the third. She decided quickly that stealing one painting worth two or three million dollars, minimum, made motive enough. She would quit while she was ahead.

She took one last look at Len—Tim Wylie—before she left the house. He looked like a piece of meat, she decided. "Murder our daughter, you bastard!" she muttered.

3

8:42 P.M.

At the motel she returned to her room through the back door, then went down to the desk and handed over her key. "If my friend shows up, tell him to go to hell," she said to the clerk.

She had paid for the room with cash. "The room's yours for the night, Barbara," said the clerk. "You've paid for it.

You know, you might find a *new* friend to share it with you." He smirked. "After midnight."

"Not tonight, lover."

The clerk's face darkened, and he nodded and said nothing more.

Now the point was to change clothes and get to the Ten Strikes Lounge as quickly as possible. She pulled into a parking lot, took a space as far out of the lights as possible, and changed. Before she left the lot, she tossed the blue jeans and sweatshirt into a Dumpster.

9:34 P.M.

"You look like a million," Sonya told her as Erika took a stool at the bar.

"I look like a hundred thousand."

Sonya grinned. "You look like a college education."

The dress Erika had changed into in the car was a hot pink mini, with a skirt five inches above her knees. She wore sheer dark stockings and shiny black shoes.

"Everything okay?" Sonya asked.

"Piece of cake. But I need a drink. I've got a long night ahead of me and no more drinks till god knows when."

Fred was behind the bar. Sonya signaled him. "Pour the lady a double Jack Daniels Black. And meet Erika Björling."

Fred brought the bottle and glass and poured in front of her. He put a glass of ice water on the side. "I'd know you anywhere," he said. "You come in one or two nights a week, drink a couple doubles of black Jack, and talk a lot with Sonya, not very often with me. You are a friend of

Sonya, as I judge, but to me you are only an acquaintance."

"And sometimes I get a little schnocked."

"And sometimes you get a little schnocked."

"You've never seen me in anything but skirts. I always show a lot of leg, and you've always noticed."

Fred nodded.

"And you don't say anything more than that," Sonya said. "When you complicate your story, they find something to trip you up. So that's all, absolutely all."

A man in a blue shirt emblazoned with the emblem of a bowling league hoisted himself on a bar stool. "How 'bout a Bud Light, Freddy?"

"You got it."

"Some nights it seems like it's not worth coming in. God, I bowled a mess!"

"And finished early. God, Mike, you are *early.*"

"Yeah?"

"Sure are. Anyway, don't stare right now, but sitting over there in the booth with Sonya—"

The man did stare right now. "Jesus Christ!"

"Right. Erika Björling. She comes in once in a while. Look at the legs."

"How could I miss 'em? You know her? Could you introduce me?"

"Maybe Sonya can. I'll ask her when she comes over."

"Hey, Linda. How'd you like to have a figure like that?"

The muscular woman, a regular bowler at Ten Strikes, glanced at the young woman in the booth, then smiled wanly and spoke to Sonya. "Erika Björling. If I've seen her once on TV, I've seen her five hundred times. Y' know, it's a damned shame that show was canceled. I mean, she was *so* good! She doesn't bowl?"

"No. Just comes in for a drink now and then."

"Looka the dress. To die for! I mean, to be able to wear it. Well . . . *you* could."

"Y' gotta feel sorry for her. She lost her daughter that awful way. Now she's out of work. Frankly, she drinks too much. You'd think she'd do her drinking in some great club, but . . . well, she comes in here and snorts a few once or twice a week. Always alone. We try to be friendly to her."

His name was Hugo, and in some way the name fit. He was a huge black man, and a joke around the alley had it that he broke pins. He drank pints of Bass Ale on draft, three or four of them without showing the slightest sign of inebriation. Another joke was that he was a piano mover and could carry a piano all by himself. In fact, he was a chiropractor.

"Well, that's for sure *some* woman," he said of Erika. "I remember her. She was a favorite of my wife's. She was a favorite of my kids. God almighty, a man wishes he could do something for her. But— I guess you can always think about it."

5

11:10 P.M.

"How much have you had to drink, for Christ sake?"

"Not enough to screw up."

"It's on television already."

"I saw."

They were in the parking lot behind the bowling alley: Grant and Erika. Furtively he transferred the van Gogh from her MG to his silver-gray Cadillac. She handed him the purse with the Colt automatic in it.

"I don't dare kiss you right now," he said. "God knows I'd like to. But if anybody saw that—"

"Anybody seeing us together is bad enough."

"So—" He took her in his arms and kissed her. "Have courage, my darling. You're going to need it. But don't lose faith. We've done it right. In the morning I'll deep-six the gun and the painting and—"

"About that time I'll be waking up in my new little cell."

"On your way to being a millionaire."

"I'll keep that in mind. It's all that's going to sustain me."

6

12:34 A.M.

Erika left the Ten Strikes Lounge reluctantly, knowing she would be in jail before the night was over.

Sonya put another martini in front of Grant. "By god, she did it!"

"If she just doesn't lose her cool."

"Well, I'm glad I'm not in her position. And not in yours, to tell you the truth. I'm in as far as I want to be."

"The only problem I have with you is your confidence in Fred."

"Fred will be no problem."

"I've relied on your word about that."

"Erika has a long night ahead of her. And sometime before dawn, she's going to be calling her lawyer. You going to stay up all night?"

He nodded. "I suppose. I know I won't be able to sleep."

"Want some TLC?"

He grinned. "I take my chief alibi witness home with me the night when—"

"We sneaked in and out of your place many, many times, and nobody saw."

"Well . . . It's going to be a long night."

"Tell me something about this long night that everybody's going to have. Did Tim Wylie *really* kill Tammy?"

Grant glanced around the bar, as if this word would somehow slip through the air and be overheard. He leaned toward Sonya and said very quietly, "I haven't the slightest idea. Erika thinks so, and that's all that counts."

FOUR

Thursday, April 13—11:39 P.M.

Officer Daniel Mulligan recognized the man in the shabby raincoat who approached in the glaring, flashing lights of four police cars and an Emergency Squad wagon.

"Hiya, Mulligan! Sorry you signed on?"

Officer Daniel Mulligan had never been sorry he had signed on with the Los Angeles Police Department. He regretted some of the duty assignments that came his way. This one in particular was a bitch. North Perugia Way. Bel Air. Murder in a mansion. It had started to drizzle, which did nothing for the patience of the reporters who insisted they had a right to go inside the house, or at least to get closer, or for the patience of the officers who literally had to push some of them back.

"Lieutenant . . . Ain't this a night?"

Lieutenant Columbo shook his head. "I'd ask the usual question, Mulligan. But I know the answer."

"The usual question?"

" 'Who got dead?' This time I know." He shook his head. "Give me another hour and a half, and it wouldn't have got to be my case. I was goin' home at midnight. I stopped in at the office, and— 'Hey, Columbo! Get up to the Tim Wylie place!' yells Cap'n Sczciegel. How 'bout you? How'd you get stuck on this one?"

Mulligan grinned and shook his head. No matter how many times he encountered Lieutenant Columbo, he was still surprised by him. The man looked like anything but what he was: a legend in the Department. Columbo broke rules other detectives dared not break—and he cleared cases other detectives could not clear.

Rain glistened on his tousled hair and his face—failing, however, to put out the fire in the butt that was left of his cigar. Water had to leak through his tattered veteran of a raincoat; but in spite of the hour and the rain, the lieutenant smiled wryly as he looked toward the house and at the array of emergency vehicles on the street and in the driveway.

"Who's inside?"

"Sergeant Ruiz and four uniformed guys. Dr. Culp. The people from the Crime Scene Unit."

"How 'bout Mrs. Wylie?"

"I understand she found the body."

Columbo sighed loudly. "Okay. Gotta get to work. Mrs. Columbo gets upset when I work a night tour and they find a body in the last half-hour. She figures those cases oughta go over to the next bunch of guys. I already cleared one case today. Body found along Stone Canyon Reservoir. Got dead of a heart attack, it turns out. Not a homicide."

"Heard the radio call on that one," said Mulligan.

" 'When constabulary's duty's to be done . . . ' " Columbo sighed. "At least I can get in out of the rain,

Mulligan. Take it easy." He tossed his cigar butt into the wet shrubbery and walked up to the door.

The body lay covered on the living-room floor. Dr. Harold Culp uncovered it for Columbo.

Tim Wylie, lying on his face, was all but unrecognizable. A bullet fired into his right ear had exited through his left eye. Besides that, an immense bloodstain had spread over the carpet, obviously from other wounds to his body.

"Before she was taken upstairs by her doctor," said Sergeant Jesús Ruiz, "Mrs. Wylie noticed that a painting was gone from the wall. The doctor said it was a van Gogh and worth at least a million dollars."

"A million or more? Must've been some picture. Robbery and murder, ya figure, Jesús?"

Columbo pronounced the sergeant's name in the Spanish way: Hay-ZOOSS. The young detective was a compact man with black, brush-cut hair, brown eyes, and an olive complexion. He was dressed neatly in a blue blazer, gray slacks, and polished black shoes.

"That's what the doctor said. A million, minimum. He's upstairs with Mrs. Wylie. He has her sedated now. Her story was that she was out playing bridge, which she does every Thursday evening, and she came home and found—"

"Y' got people searching the house?"

"Right. They're upstairs right now."

Columbo squatted beside the body. "That where a slug went?" he asked, pointing to a hole in the carpet.

Ruiz nodded. "It's in the floor. Crime Scene will have to cut a piece of the wood out to get the slug."

"Crime Scene— That's you, uh . . . You're Sergeant—"

"Davidson, Lieutenant." The sergeant in charge of the Crime Scene Unit was a stocky redheaded woman, wearing a badge on her blue blazer. She and her three people were responsible for taking photographs, taking samples of hair and fluids—blood especially—and anything else found at the scene of a crime.

"Right. Davidson. We've worked together on other cases." Columbo shook his head. "This one's messy, isn't it?"

"I've seen worse," said the sergeant.

Columbo turned to Dr. Culp. "Guess I don't need to ask how the man died. Got any idea when, Doc?"

"I knew you'd ask. I'd say he's been dead three hours, roughly."

"Meanin', like eight-thirty?"

"Based on body temperature and the onset of rigor mortis, I'd place the time of death as between, oh, eight-thirty and . . . nine. The ambient temperature—that is, room temperature—is about seventy. The body has been cooling for roughly three hours. You can't be one-hundred-percent accurate, you know." He ran a hand across the bald spot on the back of his head. "What are you doing working in the middle of the night, Columbo?"

"Same thing you are, Doc. With murder you don't get nine-to-five days and forty-hour weeks."

"Can we move him?"

Columbo turned to Sergeant Davidson. "If Crime Scene has got all the pictures it wants." The sergeant nodded. "Let's turn him over, then."

Columbo and Davidson rolled the body over gently.

The carpet underneath was stained with blood. Both of Wylie's hands had bullet holes in them.

"Whatta ya figure, 9 mm?" Columbo asked.

"7.65 mm—.32 caliber," said Sergeant Davidson.

"Ya sure?"

She nodded. "The shooter didn't bother to pick up the ejected shell casings. They were fired from an automatic.

I'd guess a Colt. The ballistics boys will be able to tell."

Columbo tugged at his ear. "Thirty-two . . . Little bitty automatic. Concealable."

"Right," said Sergeant Davidson.

"Well, Jesús— How about entry? You found any busted locks or anything like that?"

Sergeant Ruiz shook his head. "No. We've checked all the doors and windows. First thing we did."

Columbo shook his head. "Which makes it sound like he *let* somebody in." Then he turned to Dr. Culp. "If it's okay with Sergeant Davidson, you can have the body."

Summoned by Dr. Culp, two men from the coroner's office wheeled in a gurney and lifted the body of Tim Wylie.

Columbo took a fresh cigar from a pocket of his raincoat. "Seein' a cigar butt in the ashtray, I guess Mr. Wylie smoked cigars. So the smell of mine won't offend Mrs. Wylie. Anybody got a match?" One of the men from the coroner's office offered flame from his lighter. Columbo puffed for a moment. "Sure does look like somebody came to steal that painting and killed Mr. Wylie in the process. On the other hand— No break-in. That doesn't fit."

Columbo walked to the bar. He bent over the two glasses sitting there and sniffed. "Bourbon. Scotch. Glasses are full. Ice has melted in them, I betcha. Drinks poured and not a sip taken. Hey, Davidson, better have the contents of these glasses analyzed, besides checkin' 'em for fingerprints. What I'll wanta know is this: was there ice in these glasses? If yes, then we know the murder didn't happen within the past hour and a half, say. It'd take ice cubes that long to melt."

"Right," said Sergeant Carol Davidson.

"Looka this. The cap's loose on the Scotch bottle. Just barely on there. Gotta think of another scenario. Mr. Wylie let somebody in. Somebody he knew. Poured two drinks, but before either of them could take a sip—bang! And it's gotta be the person he poured a drink for, doesn't it? Otherwise there'd be two bodies."

A man came in. Bustled in. He was white-haired, flushed of face, and he glared at the LAPD team with an air of condescension and impatience.

"I'm Dr. Gilbert Haas. Who's in charge?"

"Lieutenant Columbo. Homicide. LAPD."

Dr. Haas nodded crisply at the odd-looking detective. "Mrs. Wylie is my patient. I must insist that she not be disturbed tonight. Your people will have to stay out of her room and leave her alone. Needless to say, she's in shock. Besides, she's seventy years old. I have her sedated. Her daughter will arrive shortly. I'll stay until she does."

"Who called you, Doctor?" Columbo asked.

"Mrs. Wylie called me."

"Are you familiar with this house?"

Dr. Haas nodded.

"You see the place on the walls where the painting is gone?" Columbo asked.

"Whoever did this," said the doctor, "knew exactly what he was here for. Any one of those paintings was worth a million dollars. The van Gogh that's missing could have been worth two or three million. Somebody knew the value of priceless art."

"You'd guess, then," said Columbo, "that Mr. Wylie surprised a burglar—or two burglars—in the act of stealing that picture. Caught, they killed him and took the picture."

"That is precisely what I would surmise," Dr. Haas said coldly.

"You say those two others there are worth a million apiece?"

"Easily. The missing painting is *"Printemps du verger"*

by Vincent van Gogh. The title means "Springtime in the Orchard." The one on the left there is *"Entrer en danse,"* by Henri de Toulouse-Lautrec, and the one on the right is *"Harlequins nus,"* by Pablo Picasso."

"I'm gonna lose sleep over this until I figure out why a burglar would kill a man and then take one painting and leave two million worth of others hanging there. That doesn't make sense, does it, Doctor?"

"Well, I'll leave you to lose sleep over it, Lieutenant. My concern is my patient."

"Was Mr. Wylie your patient, too?"

"Yes. For many years."

"Was he in good health, generally?"

"Very good for a man his age."

"Didn't use drugs by any chance?"

"Absolutely not."

"You would have known?"

"I would have known."

"Well, thank ya, Doctor. I hope I don't have to ask you any more questions."

One of the uniformed officers had come into the room. His name tag said he was Heath. He was carrying a piece of paper, carrying it gingerly, holding it by one corner.

"What ya got?"

Heath put the note down on the escritoire at one end of the room, and Columbo sat down and read it.

Tim, you are an evil bastard! I know now what happened to Tammy. A man who would kidnap and murder his own daughter is— Well, I don't know what to call you. I hope you can live with it. Actually, I hope you can't. Keep an eye out for who's behind you.

Erika

Columbo got up and made room for Ruiz and Davidson to read the note. Dr. Haas couldn't restrain his curiosity and stepped up to read it, too.

"Erika . . . Tammy . . . Uhhm . . . Lessee . . . What was that case? Tammy disappeared. They found her body out in a canyon. She was the daughter of . . . Erika Björling. Right?"

"My god!" Davidson exclaimed. "She's accusing Wylie of having killed *his daughter!*"

"Yeah. We never knew who Tammy's father was. Erika wouldn't say, and nobody ever figured it out."

"This is an *outrageous* accusation!" Dr. Haas protested. "Tim Wylie had an impeccable reputation. An accusation like this could have ruined him. I'd suggest to you, Lieutenant, that this note may well represent an attempt at blackmail." The doctor showed a twisted, bitter smile. "In any case, Tim had a vasectomy ten years ago."

"Tammy was born nineteen or twenty years ago," said Sergeant Davidson.

"I don't believe it," the doctor insisted. "I don't give a damn; I don't believe it."

"There's a way to find out," Columbo said. He turned to Dr. Culp, who was sitting on a couch watching and listening. "Take a good blood sample for DNA testing, Doc. We may want to exhume the body of Tammy Björling and get a tissue sample for a DNA match."

"I suppose when one is murdered, he and his family are subjected to all sorts of intrusive procedures," remarked Dr. Haas.

"Well, Sir, we do like to find out who kills people and why."

"Yes. I'm sure you do. I'll go back upstairs to my patient. The daughter, Mrs. Glassman, will be here soon. I hope there won't be any problem about her getting in."

"No problem. Jesús, the man outside in the rain is Mulligan. Would you step out and tell him to be looking for Mrs. Glassman?"

The doctor went up the stairs.

"Uhh . . . Tell me somethin', Heath. You found this note. Did you find the envelope?"

"No, Sir. We've been going through the trash, too. About a week's trash is still in the house, from the look of it. You notice there's no date on the note, so it could have been around here a long time."

Columbo frowned at the note. "Doesn't seem like somethin' a man'd want to save."

"We'll check it for fingerprints," said Sergeant Davidson.

"Right."

When Mulligan knocked on the door and came in to say Mrs. Glassman was outside, Columbo suggested he take her in the back door and up the back stairs. Her father's body was still in the house, and his blood still gleamed on the floor and carpet. Columbo went back to say hello.

Victoria Wylie Glassman was a handsome, well-put-together woman of thirty-five or so.

"My condolences, Ma'am. I won't trouble you with any questions, except maybe you could answer just one."

"I have no idea, Lieutenant Columbo. My father was liked by everyone."

"Uh . . . I'm sure he was. My question is, what kind of liquor did he drink?"

"Scotch."

"Thank ya, Ma'am. That's helpful information."

She paused in the kitchen. She was a big woman, taller than Columbo: a dishwater blond with a wide mouth. "So

long as we've confronted each other, do you have any idea
who did it? Or why?"

"No, Ma'am, I haven't. A valuable painting is missing,
but the house wasn't broken into, and your father seems to
have poured a couple of drinks just before he was killed.
We thought burglary, but it doesn't seem quite that simple."

"Is my mother asleep?"

"I'd guess so. Dr. Haas said he had her sedated."

Victoria Glassman sat down on the stool where the maid
sat at the kitchen counter to peel vegetables. "Can somebody bring *me* a Scotch?"

"The bottle has to be dusted for fingerprints, but if
there's another bottle—"

"There'll be another. Underneath the bar."

Officer Heath had overheard and went to bring the
bottle.

"Lieutenant . . . You're going to find out something my
father managed to keep secret for years. So—"

"Does it have anything to do with Miss Erika Björling?"

"Damn! You're sharp, Lieutenant Columbo. How'd you
figure that out already?"

"I didn't. We found a letter written to him by Miss Björling."

"She was only one of many, and her affair with him goes
back many, many years."

"Did she have a child by him?"

Victoria Glassman blanched. *"My god! You don't mean
Tammy!* You don't mean Tammy Björling was my half
sister?"

"Miss Björling says so."

"No . . . It could have been any of a dozen men. Any of
a score. Erika is a slut, Lieutenant! She slept all over town.
What did she do in this letter, demand money?"

Columbo shook his head. "It's gonna come out. We

can't keep it a secret. She accused your father of killing Tammy."

"Then she killed my father! She came here and killed my father!"

"I'm gonna look into that possibility, Ma'am."

2

Friday, April 14—1:09 A.M.

Erika lived in an apartment building in Van Nuys. When Columbo arrived and rang her bell, she did not answer. He went out to the black-and-white he had followed to the address.

"Okay, Mulligan, lemme have your mike."

Patrolman Mulligan, whom Columbo had rescued from duty in the rain outside the Wylie house, handed over the radio microphone.

"Center, this is Unit Four-oh-Four. Lieutenant Columbo speakin'. I need a telephone-authorized search warrant and an arrest warrant. Reasonable cause to believe murder was committed by the resident of this address. That's the Tim Wylie murder. Need that toot dee sweet, if you can get it for me. Officer Mulligan will fill you in on the name and address. Also, since I'm probably going to have to arrest a female here, send me a unit with a female officer, if ya please."

He walked back to his car, the Peugeot, and checked the piece of plastic he had thrown over the top to keep the rain from leaking through a couple of rents in the canvas. He was going to have to have that fixed one of these days.

Usually, in a case like this, a night-duty Assistant DA could get a warrant by telephone, from a night-duty magistrate. In the old days you didn't bother with stuff like that. These days, it was a good idea to bother. They'd set up procedures so an officer could get a warrant in minutes, then do the paperwork in the morning. Mulligan would get the search-and-arrest authorization by radio, and then they could move in.

Another black-and-white pulled up behind the Peugeot. The driver was the woman officer he'd asked for.

"Hiya. Lieutenant Columbo. Homicide. Y' may have to arrest a celebrity here."

The officer nodded. "Lieutenant. I'm Patricia Finn, Van Nuys. Got the call from downtown."

Columbo ran his hand through his hair and flipped away rainwater. "The worst part is, this is not my tour. It'll teach me to stay away from the center if I want to get home at a decent hour. Incidentally, I'm workin' on the Tim Wylie murder. Erika Björling lives here."

"My god, is *she* a suspect?"

"May be, dependin' on how she answers a question or three."

FIVE

Friday, April 14—1:09 A.M.

The warrants came by radio, and Columbo could have entered the Björling apartment; but he decided to wait outside until Erika Björling appeared. If she didn't appear in thirty minutes or so, he would enter anyway.

Officer Patricia Finn was an interesting woman: of somewhat slighter build than the typical female officer of LAPD but visibly muscular and self-assured. Her face was long and thin, her hair mousy brown, and her hazel eyes mobile and foxy.

He lit a cigar while they waited. She lit a cigarette. "I've heard of you, Lieutenant. I suppose everybody in the Department has heard of you."

"Not guilty," said Columbo.

"Do we really have a case against Erika Björling? I mean, my god, did *she* kill Tim Wylie?"

"Well . . . Finn, you know how it is. Ya gotta check out everything. There may be better ways of figuring out cases, but I haven't found any yet. Who was it said something about how something was one percent inspiration and ninety-nine percent perspiration?"

"Edison said that about invention."

"Yeah. That's right. I always remember that, except I sometimes forget who said it about what. But that's important to keep in mind. It must be great to be smart. I wish I was. I have to do my job by—" He stopped and shook his head. "I have to work hard, check out every little thing. What I'd rather be doin' right now is sleeping at home in bed. But— Well, this thing has got to be checked out."

"I'm hoping to become a detective."

"Well, good luck to ya. If there's anything I can do to help, let me know. Be glad to put in a word with Cap'n Sczciegel for you."

Finn smiled. "I'm afraid the first thing I have to do is pass a civil-service examination."

"Oh, yeah. I guess that's right. They got things all organized these days, haven't they? You pass your qualification at the firin' range?"

"Yes, Sir. I have."

"That always gives me trouble. I gotta get out there one of these days and—"

2

1:27 A.M.

Just before one-thirty, a green MG pulled into the garage adjacent to the apartment building. Columbo and Finn walked in.

"Miss Björling? Miss Erika Björling?"

"Yes."

Columbo's first impression was that this exquisitely beautiful woman could not have committed murder. She had about her a delicacy that had not shown on the television screen. In a pink mini-dress and showing shapely legs in dark stockings, she looked like anything but a person who would have paused to put a final shot into the ear of a man she had just felled with .32 slugs.

"I'm Lieutenant Columbo, LAPD Homicide. This is Officer Finn. We have a warrant for your arrest, Miss Björling. I'm kinda hoping we can settle the matter and we won't have to arrest you."

"Arrest me for *what?*"

"For the murder of Mr. Tim Wylie."

She blanched. "I heard on the news that— My god! How could you think *I* did it? *Why* would I do it?"

"Can we go inside your apartment, Miss Björling? We've got a warrant to search it."

Erika Björling glanced from Columbo to Finn and back. "Can I say no? What if I said no?"

"I'm afraid we'd have to do it anyway," Columbo said. "A team of officers."

Erika turned and stared at four uniformed officers who had now entered the garage. Her jaw trembled, and she pointed toward the door.

Inside her apartment, Erika poured herself a drink, though she was already wobbly. She sat down on the couch in her living room and watched policemen work through her rooms, opening drawers and closets, intruding into everything.

"Miss Björling, I have to ask you a question," Columbo said grimly. "You lost your daughter some years ago. She was kidnapped and murdered."

"The worst thing that ever happened to me in my life," Erika mumbled.

"I have to ask you who was Tammy's father."

Erika shook her head convulsively. "I don't know."

"Well . . . We have an idea who it was. We can get a court order to exhume Tammy's body and get DNA that we can match against Tim Wylie's."

"No! No! You leave her alone. If you have to do something like that, I can give you a snip of her hair. That has DNA in it. But . . . Why? What. . . ? "

One of the uniformed officers came to Columbo, bent over, and quietly told him something.

"I'd like to change the subject, Miss Björling. If I can. Where have you been all evening?"

"I was here until . . . I don't know when, exactly. I guess about eight. I was lonely and didn't have anything to do, so I drove down to the Ten Strikes Lounge for a couple of drinks."

"Where's that?"

"It's in Long Beach."

Columbo smiled and scratched his head. "That's a long way to go for a couple of drinks, isn't it?"

"It sure is. But I have friends there."

"What time did you leave here?"

"Well . . . I got to the Ten Strikes about nine. I go down the San Diego Freeway, and it's got to be—what?— twenty-five or thirty miles. Depending on traffic, it takes almost an hour to get there. So I suppose I left here a little after eight. Something like that."

"When did you stop answering your telephone, Miss Björling?"

"I always answer my telephone."

"Well, you didn't answer it at 7:00, and you didn't answer it at 7:22, or at 7:38, which are all before the time you say you left. Calls from those times are on your answering machine."

Erika shrugged. "So? I was probably in the shower. Or— Oh, yeah, I ran out for a can of soup."

"When you got out of the shower and came back from buying soup, were there calls on your answering machine?"

"You say there were."

"You didn't check?"

"I don't always. I'm not a slave to the telephone. Anyway, what the hell? What difference does it make?"

"Well, the medical examiner places the time of Mr. Wylie's death between eight-thirty and nine, roughly."

"I was at the Ten Strikes before nine."

"And witnesses saw you there?"

"Sure. I go there every week, sometimes twice a week. The woman who manages it is a friend of mine. When I'm feeling all alone and want somebody to talk to— The bartender knows me, too."

Columbo nodded solemnly. "The times here get a little sticky, Miss Björling. You say you left here at eight. Your telephone recorder suggests you weren't here after seven. Well—Not so big a discrepancy, I suppose. The warrant for your arrest was issued on the basis of something else. You can refuse to do what I'm about to ask you to do, but would you mind giving me a sample of your handwriting?"

Erika shrugged. "Why not? Your men searching my home will find a grocery list, my telephone list . . . Sure. What do you want me to write on, and with?"

"Uh— Uh, Finn. Gotta a pen and pad?"

Officer Finn tore a sheet from her notebook and handed it to Erika, together with a ballpoint pen.

"What you want me to write?"

"If you don't mind, write 'I know what happened to Tammy.' "

Erika frowned, but she wrote. Columbo took the sheet and studied it. "You did *know* Mr. Wylie, didn't you?"

Erika sighed. "Biblically," she said. "If you do the DNA test, you'll find out."

"Okay. Well, he was killed by someone he knew. He let the person in. The house wasn't broken into."

"None of this makes it me."

"But there's something else," said Columbo. "Miss Björling, we found in Mr. Wylie's house a note signed 'Erika' and accusing Mr. Wylie of kidnapping and murdering Tammy. Also, it sort of threatens Mr. Wylie. On the basis of that evidence, the arrest warrant was issued, and I'm afraid I'm gonna have to execute that warrant. I'm sorry."

Erika blinked. "You mean I'm under arrest? You mean I'm going to *jail?*"

"I'm afraid so. Officer Finn will read you your rights and take you into custody."

"No!"

Officer Patricia Finn spoke to Erika. "Take it easy, Miss Björling. No one ever died of being arrested. Now listen to me. 'You are under arrest. You have a right to remain silent. If you make any statement, whatever you say will be taken down as evidence and may be used against you. You have a right to be represented by an attorney. If you cannot afford an attorney, one will be appointed for you at public expense.' Do you understand your rights?"

Erika nodded. She mumbled, "Yes."

Officer Finn pulled a pair of handcuffs from the pouch on her belt. "Turn around please. Behind your back."

Erika began to cry as her hands were locked behind her. "Jesus Christ!" she sobbed. "I'm not a murderer! You've all seen me on television. Hey! How could you believe I could kill someone?"

SIX

Friday, April 14—2:39 A.M.

Officer Finn took Erika to Sybil Brand Institute, the Los Angeles County jail for women. She demanded to be allowed to make a telephone call. She called Grant Kellogg.

"Are they listening?" she asked him. "Is this call private?"

"Absolutely private," he told her. "If they want to lose a case for sure, all they have to do is listen to prisoners' conversations with lawyers."

"Prisoner— Right. That's me. I guess I'll be locked up in a little while." Her voice broke. "I was brought in here in handcuffs, hands behind my back. What more have I got to go through? Fingerprinting, mug shots . . . and strip search, I suppose."

"Don't let it get to you. Standard procedure, like I told you. Any surprises?"

"No. They bought the note. And they bought the calls you and Sonya put on my answering machine, which of course made it sound like I was lying about the time I left the house."

"Who arrested you?"

"A *nut!* Some slovenly bastard in a tattered raincoat, that—"

"Erika. Are you talking about Lieutenant Columbo?"

"Right. Columbo."

"Did you talk to him, much?"

"No. Not much. I played the innocent."

"Well, just remember this. Columbo is maybe the shrewdest, smartest homicide detective in Los Angeles. Does he know you'll be represented by me?"

"I told him who I was calling."

"Hey, kid! Couldn't be better. The story suddenly got worth twice what it was. The best homicide detective LA has got against the best defense lawyer in town!"

"But, Jesus Christ! Will he—?"

"Figure it out? Get you convicted? No way! He's got a problem to solve, and he doesn't know the answer. *We* know the answer. We know *all* the answers."

"I'm scared, Grant."

"You're scared of the trappings. The handcuffs, the strip search, the—"

"You warned me about those things. But I'm scared this guy's gonna figure it out."

"*Honey, baby!* We wouldn't have done it if we weren't sure. You just relax now. This is the hell part for you. Just sleep with thoughts of how rich you're going to be."

"I'll try, Grant. I'll try. But, Jesus, this is tough! Sleep? Where'll I be? In a cell? How could I sleep?"

"This is the worst night. After tonight it gets easier. Believe me—it does."

2

9:28 A.M.

Except for the night when Tammy disappeared and the agonizing nights afterward, it was the worst night Erika had ever known in her life. They booked her on the charge of murder and advised her that she would be held without bail. They took her mug shots, then fingerprinted her, then ordered her to strip and submit to a humiliating and painful search of every orifice of her body. They handed her a pair of blue dungarees and a pair of white sneakers. When she was dressed, they led her to a cell and locked her in for what remained of the night.

She did not sleep. Not for a moment. She had no idea of what time it was but supposed it was early in the morning when a woman came pushing a stainless-steel cart, poured her a tin cup of black coffee, and handed it and a stale doughnut through the bars. Erika ate the doughnut and drank the coffee. In addition to everything else, she had a hangover and thought she might have to vomit in the toilet.

A long time later, another woman, this one in uniform, came to her cell. "Erika Björling, right?" The burly woman shook her head. "I've seen you a thousand times on the TV. Never thought I'd see you in here."

"I never thought I'd be in here," said Erika.

"You're going to be with us for a while. You'll stay in this cell for a few days. There's some orientation. Interviews to decide just where you belong in here. Medical exams and so on. Then you'll be assigned to a dormitory and a work detail. You can make phone calls to your family or to your lawyer. You have any questions?"

Erika leaned against the bars and sobbed. "What I want to know is, where the hell *is* my lawyer?"

3

9:37 A.M.

He was where she might have expected him to be. He was twenty miles out to sea, on his boat *Excalibur*. Though the rain had stopped, the Pacific was still running rough. On another morning he would not have ventured out into this weather. But he was an experienced boatman and had no fear of the seas *Excalibur* climbed and plunged over.

Visibility was poor from the small boat. Once, from the top of a wave, he spotted a tanker. It was only after he had climbed two more waves that he was able to determine just how to avoid it. It passed a hundred yards from his altered course, so he'd been in no real danger. But he'd had to alter *his* course. With whatever goodwill, the tanker could not have changed course fast enough to avoid running him over if he had remained in its path.

He was out far enough and out of sight from everything and everyone. He tossed the Colt automatic overboard. He didn't even bother to handle it with gloves. They'd never find it in a million years. *He* couldn't have found it, even if he'd wanted to. He tossed a box of ammunition after it.

The next toss was more difficult. The van Gogh was worth more than he and Erika would make from this caper. The morning newspapers were saying it was worth four million dollars at a minimum. But he *could not* risk keeping it. It had to be the hottest piece of property in the world, right now. No way could he fence it.

Almost as bad as throwing into the sea a property worth that much money was the sense that he made himself a philistine, destroying a work of art the whole world cherished. But there was nothing for it. His life—and Erika's—depended on it.

He had prepared. It was in a canvas bag, chained to a concrete block. He lifted it, shook his head sadly, and heaved it over the side.

Noon.

In bed at 4:00 a.m., up at 10:00, Columbo had eaten a couple of hard-boiled eggs with his coffee as he looked over the morning papers.

BELOVED ACTOR KILLED IN ROBBERY!
TIM WYLIE BELIEVED VICTIM OF ART THIEVES, BUT TV PERSONALITY ARRESTED, JAILED

After a stop at headquarters, Columbo found himself hungry and tense. It wasn't going to be a short or easy day, so he went by Burt's for lunch: chili and a game or three of nine-ball.

"Do I know Columbo, or do I know Columbo?"

Uh-oh. Adrienne Boswell. Journalist. Smart, tough, and impossible to avoid. She was playing pool with one of Burt's regulars, though not eating a bowl of Burt's chili. She knew where to find him. A hundred reporters in LA were looking for him, but Adrienne knew where to look.

There was no getting around it, Columbo had to admit. Adrienne was some kind of woman. She was beating the guy at pool. She even beat *him* sometimes. Right now she was the center of attention at Burt's. Her worn and faded blue jeans—*genuinely* faded—were tight. Her gray UCLA sweatshirt was loose. Her flaming red hair lay around her shoulders. Her green eyes laughed as she grinned at Columbo.

"Hiya, Adrienne. You here lookin' for me?"

"Oh, no. I came in to play pool." She lowered her voice and muttered, "And get stared at. Hey, Columbo. If there's a famous case, you get it. How you manage that?"

For once he took off his raincoat and hung it on a hook. "Gimme my choice, I'd do only the obscure ones."

She kissed him warmly on the cheek. "A thousand reporters wish they knew where to find you. They gotta learn to play pool. Right?"

"And eat the best chili in LA."

"I wish I could get Dan to try it," she said. "It might make a better man of him."

"Does he need to be a better man?"

Adrienne nudged him with an elbow. "Hey, Columbo. You know I love the guy, even if he doesn't appreciate real chili. So ask me no questions, I'll tell you no lies."

"Ask me questions, I'll tell you all the lies I can think of. I can't talk about the Wylie case."

"Hey. You've got Erika Björling in jail. You've got a van Gogh worth four million dollars missing. You can't just say, 'No, I'm not gonna talk.' It's the most famous case in the country!"

"Figure so?"

"Okay. Background, Columbo. Off the record." She looked at him from the corner of her eye and lifted her chin. "You don't really think Erika killed Wylie, do you?"

He picked up a cue. The man who had been playing had eased away. "Some stuff about it's a little too simple," he said. "Too easy. I don't like cases that are too easy."

"Doesn't give you a chance to be detective. What would be Erika's motive?"

"Can't say right now."

"I mean, she wouldn't want to steal the van Gogh, would she?"

Columbo shrugged. "What's a thief gonna do with a van Gogh? He couldn't sell it. It's the most notorious stolen art in the world right now."

"And some Arabs and some Japanese don't give a damn," Adrienne said. She racked the balls to start a new game of nine-ball. "Private collectors—"

"Mr. Wylie didn't seem to give a damn, either. He had other paintings worth millions. Imagine keeping stuff that valuable in a house without an alarm system."

"Pulling the painting off the wall should have set off an alarm."

"Well, it didn't. There wasn't any."

"Then—Columbo, Tim Wylie was about as big a celebrity as there is in this country. But I never heard he was a collector of priceless art. Maybe he figured he didn't have to protect it because nobody knew he had it."

"Somebody knew," Columbo said dryly.

"Right. And maybe that limits the community of suspects," said Adrienne. She broke the balls. The three went in, but the cue ball was left behind the six. She shot the cue ball down the table to the rail. It bounced back and hit the one gently, leaving Columbo a shot—but nothing easy. "You could almost say it had to be somebody who'd been in the house before. Well— Not actually. But it's a departure, isn't it?"

"You missed your callin', Adrienne. You shoulda been a cop."

Burt put two bowls of chili and two Dr. Peppers on the

shelf behind the pool table. Columbo opened two cellophane-wrapped packages of crackers and crushed them into his chili. He ate a little before he moved up to the table for a shot on the one-ball.

"You missed yours," said Adrienne. "You should've been a gourmet chef."

"I'm an aficionado of chili. But I like a lot of other good stuff. I like anything that comes out of the ocean."

"So, okay. What do you have against Erika Björling?"

"Can't discuss. Ask the DA."

"Columbo—"

"Uhmm?"

"Do you figure he knew the person who killed him?"

Columbo studied the array of balls on the table. "Now, that I can't say, Ma'am. That I can't say."

"The chief of police made a statement this morning. He says the house wasn't broken into."

"So Mr. Wylie let somebody in, I guess." Columbo shot at the one-ball. The shot was too tough, and he didn't make it.

Adrienne banked the one-ball two rails and sank it. Clear now, she ran the table and won the game. She grinned at Columbo. "Damn. We forgot to bet."

"Dollar a game," he said, shoving a dollar bill onto the table.

"Columbo . . . There's something wrong with this case, isn't there? I can't guess what motive Erika Björling had for wanting Wylie dead, but whatever it was, it's inconsistent with the theft of a priceless work of art. It doesn't fit together, does it?"

Columbo racked the pool balls. "You figured that out already?"

SEVEN

1

Friday, April 14—2:42 P.M.

As Grant Kellogg walked into Sybil Brand, he was besieged by newspeople.

"Will you be representing Erika Björling?"

"She called me. We're going to talk about it. And that's all I can say at this point."

"One question, Mr. Kellogg. Do you *know* Miss Björling?"

"I do. We've been friends for years. Now— I may have something more to say after I've talked to her."

Forty minutes later, when he came out, he *did* have something more to say. "I spent more than half an hour talking with Miss Björling, and I tell you on her behalf that she is absolutely innocent. She did not murder Tim Wylie, and she has no idea who did, or why. In fact, she is quite confused—as I am, frankly—as to why the police should charge *her* with this crime when the motive for it is absolutely clear. I hope the police are making every effort to find the missing Van Gogh, which, at last appraisal, is valued at four-point-seven million dollars. Miss Björling has asked me to work with the District Attorney to have this case resolved as quickly as possible. If the case has to go to trial, she is confident, as I am, that she will be acquitted, so we want to get it over with as soon as possible, so she does not have to sit in jail one day longer than necessary."

"Can you describe her mental state, Mr. Kellogg? Is she upset?"

"*Of course,* she's upset. She has been accused of a murder she didn't commit. She is in jail, which she has never been before. It's an extremely stressful thing, but I think I can say she is bearing it bravely."

"Did Erika Björling and Tim Wylie know each other?"

"I'll have something to say about that, maybe, a few days from now."

"Did *you* know Tim Wylie?"

"I met him."

"What will be the basis of the defense?"

"I don't know yet. It will of course be that she was not near his house last night and could not possibly have killed him. More than that, I can't say."

3:04 P.M.

King's Court Motel was on Sunset Boulevard. Columbo arrived there shortly after three. He pinched the fire out of his cigar and deposited it in his raincoat pocket.

"Hiya. Your name Logan?"

"I'm Dave Logan," said the desk clerk. He was a slender young man, probably not more than twenty-five, with narrow eyes and thin white lips. "What can I do for you?"

"Lieutenant Columbo. LAPD Homicide. You called."

"Oh . . . yeah, Lieutenant. I sure did. There's nothing in the papers, nothing on television, but the Wylie murder. The stories are that you arrested Erika Björling. Well— She was here last night. I'm almost sure the woman who was here was Erika Björling. I thought you'd want to know."

"Tell me about it."

"Okay. She checked in about seven o'clock, under the name Barbara Collier. Here's her card. It may have her fingerprints on it. She paid for her room in advance, with cash. A little before nine—say a quarter till—she came down, tossed her key on the desk, and said she was leaving. She said if the guy who was supposed to meet her came in, I should tell him to go to hell."

"What room did she have?"

"She had 214. For about two hours, or a little less."

"Was the room cleaned up?"

Logan nodded. "I'm afraid it was. It was vacant, and we could use it, so I told housekeeping to clean it up. In fact, it was taken by other guests about ten."

"You feel pretty sure it was her?"

"I've seen twenty or thirty pictures of her, on television and in the papers. Glamour shots, though. I—"

"Take a look at this," Columbo said. He handed Logan a mug shot taken last night at Sybil Brand. In that a scowling and deglamorized Erika Björling stared blankly at the camera.

"Oh, yeah! Oh, yeah. That's her. She had on jeans and a sweatshirt, but that's the woman who checked in here last night as Barbara Collier. No doubt about it."

"And left about a quarter to nine?"

"Right. About a quarter till nine. I could be off five minutes or so, but not more."

"Well, that's very interesting, Mr. Logan. It could have a big impact on the case. I thank ya."

3:24 P.M.

Columbo noted that it took him eleven minutes to drive from the motel to the Wylie home. He pulled his Peugeot into the driveway and got out to face one of the uniformed officers who were on duty keeping back the crowd that pressed as close as it could to the fence and driveway of the estate.

"Hiya. Don't think we've met. Lieutenant Columbo. Homicide."

The officer nodded. "We've never met formally, Lieutenant, but I've seen you around and know who you are."

"Well, thank ya . . . uh—" He stared at the officer's name tag. "Thank ya, Griffin." He glanced at the crowd. "Enough to make ya sick, isn't it?"

"Humanity . . . ," said Griffin.

Columbo could sympathize with news types; they had a job to do. The morbid didn't. Some other people with a job to do—hot-dog vendors, vendors of tacky souvenirs of Tim Wylie, hastily made but not cheap, preachers of the awful lesson taught by this death—attracted no sympathy from these two policemen who had seen it all before.

Wherever television cameras went, placards appeared urging people to read John something-or-other. Paparazzi with long lenses prowled the area, looking for the chance to capture some celebrity on film—preferably showing some embarrassing expression or posture or gesture.

Columbo tossed his cigar into the street. "Gotta go in and face the widow," he said.

"At least you don't have to tell her the man is dead," said Griffin.

"Toughest duty that goes with this job."

Griffin shook his head. "Telling a woman her husband's dead? Wait till you have to tell a mother her child is dead."

"Griffin, I've been around. I've had to do that, too."

The uniformed officer saluted. Columbo walked toward the house, slapping ash off his raincoat, then pulling on the knot in his tie.

Victoria Glassman answered the door. She was wearing cream-white leggings and a turquoise linen tunic.

"Lieutenant Columbo, Ma'am. LAPD Homicide. We met last night.

"Come in, Lieutenant," she said quietly.

"I'm sorry to have to bother you, but—"

"We understand. My mother is sitting by the pool."

It was immediately apparent to Columbo that the woman sitting by the pool was blanked out by something she had swallowed or something her doctor had injected. Her pupils were too big. She stared into the distance. She wore a tailored blue bathrobe.

He disliked making judgments of people, particularly of women; still, it was an essential of his job to be observant, and he observed—Faye had not aged as well as her husband had. Aging was more difficult for women. On men's faces, wrinkles were called "lines"; on women's faces, they were called "wrinkles." When the flesh around men's jaws slackened, it was said they were developing character. When it happened to women, they were just growing old. This woman had had her face lifted, maybe more than once, and it was apparent. She'd had her face sandpapered, or whatever it was they did, to make it smooth; and that was altogether too apparent.

"Mother, this is Lieutenant Columbo. He's the detective in charge of investigating Dad's death."

"I can't tell you how sorry I am to have to be here, Mrs. Wylie. It'd have been better if you'd never had to meet me."

Faye Wylie glanced briefly at Columbo, then resumed her fixed stare. "I want you to find out who did it," she murmured.

"I'm sure gonna try, Ma'am. All of us are."

"Do you have any ideas, Lieutenant?" asked Victoria Glassman.

"I'm afraid not much. We've got Miss Björling in jail, but it's hard to get around the conclusion that Mr. Wylie was attacked by burglars."

"Why would you want to get around that conclusion?"

"I don't know. Some way it just seems too easy. And there are some inconsistencies in the case. I'm always bothered by inconsistencies."

"Like what, Lieutenant?"

"Like that there doesn't seem to have been a forced entry, as if Mr. Wylie opened the door and let the burglars in. But why would he do that? It's like he let in somebody he knew."

"If I follow you, you're suggesting someone—like maybe Erika Björling—had another motive for killing him and took the painting to make the case look like burglary."

"Seems possible, Ma'am. That's one possibility I've got to consider."

A uniformed maid arrived carrying a silver tray. Victoria Glassman poured coffee.

"I'm sorry to have to ask questions, but I don't know any other way to find out who killed Mr. Wylie."

"I can't think of any way either, Lieutenant," Victoria said dryly.

"Well . . . In the first place, was the art insured?"

"Mother?"

Faye shook her head.

"I think the reason is, Dad didn't want to have the paintings appraised. In the first place, he didn't want to know how much they were worth. He said it would make him nervous. In the second place, he thought having appraisers and insurance agents see them would cause publicity about them. He supposed the best way to protect them against theft was to have nobody but friends know he had them."

"When we had the living room painted and the floor refinished, he took them down," Faye said dully.

"I was expecting to ask an insurance adjuster for this information," said Columbo, "but since there isn't going to be one, I have to ask if you have the exact names and maybe dates of the paintings. Also, do you know where he bought them and what he paid for them?"

"We can write a description of them," said Faye.

"I can do better than that," said Victoria. "Six or eight years ago, when Dad was out on location somewhere, I hired a professional photographer to come here and make high-quality photographs of all the paintings. I knew Dad didn't want it done, but I felt it should be. I have an album of all those pictures."

"I don't know where he bought them," Faye said. "Len would just come home with a picture—sort of grinning sheepishly—and hang it on the wall."

"Could I borrow that album, Mrs. Glassman? It'd help if we could circulate copies of the photo of the missing painting. You know, to other police departments, to art dealers, and so on."

"It's at home. Would you like to stop by and pick it up? If so, when."

"If you won't mind my comin' on Sunday, I'll stop by on Sunday afternoon."

"Lieutenant . . . The *funeral* is Sunday afternoon."

"Oh. Forgive me, both of you. I've been so busy chasin' around, asking questions, I— Well, I'm sorry."

"That's alright, Lieutenant Columbo. Make it Monday afternoon. And I'll bring the album here. We'll see you here, at, say, two or so?"

"I'll be here. And, uh, look— I know this is a strain, and I don't want to take too much of your time this morning, so I'll just raise one more subject. Do either of you know of any reason besides the burglary why somebody'd want to harm Mr. Wylie? Did he have any enemies?"

Faye lowered her head and sobbed.

Victoria spoke. "I don't think Dad had an enemy in the world. I never knew anybody who didn't like him. Not everyone was a fan of his film work, but nobody disliked him."

Columbo nodded. "That's the way I always heard. I've seen many of his pictures myself, and he always seemed to me like the most likable, most honorable man in the world."

Faye settled a steady gaze on him for a moment. "I hope you don't find out the contrary, Lieutenant Columbo."

EIGHT

Friday, April 14—4:41 P.M.

Columbo had promised to be home in time for dinner. He had a list of people to see, though, and if he could interview one more—

"Mrs. Coleridge? I'm Lieutenant Columbo. I called."

The woman in the doorway of an apartment on California Avenue opened the door wider and welcomed him in. He knew her age was seventy, roughly the same age as Faye Wylie—which made sense, because she was one of the women who played bridge with Faye every Thursday evening.

"I'm Letitia Coleridge. Come in."

This woman conspicuously shared with Faye a determination not to surrender to her threescore years and ten. He had checked her history before he came here. The fact was, she was almost exactly the same age Marilyn Monroe would have been if Marilyn Monroe were still alive—and *there* was a hard fact to believe, that MM would be sixty-nine. Letitia Coleridge might well have achieved the success Marilyn had achieved. She had the same assets.

She had once been blond. He had seen pictures of her as a blond. Sometime she had given it up, and her hair now was light brown. Her eyebrows were plucked into thin arches, darkened with mascara. She wore eye shadow and some sort of foundation makeup that smoothed her complexion. Her full lips were highlighted by pink lipstick. She had not undergone the plastic surgery that would have removed the wattle under her chin.

She wore a tight pink sweater, thrust out by breasts he had to guess were supported by nylon and rubber, and a pair of knit khaki slacks.

"I'm sorry to bother you, Ma'am."

"Au contraire," she said. "How often do I receive a visit from a homicide detective? It will relieve the boredom that has been my lot the past twenty years. Sit down. Anticipating you, I've made a pitcher of martinis."

"I . . . Well, just one maybe. I won't be here long. I just have one or two questions. Nothin' really important. Just clearing up a minor point or two."

She left him alone while she went into the kitchen of her small apartment and returned with a pitcher and two glistening stem glasses.

"I have anticipated your question. Was Faye with me and the others from, say, seven-thirty until, say, eleven, last night. She was. That's what you want to know, isn't it? If she was with us, she couldn't have killed him."

"I didn't really think she had, Ma'am."

"Oh, you had to wonder! *'Cherchez la femme.'* The wife is always a suspect." Letitia paused to smile. "I played too many femmes fatales. I could have had the Marilyn Monroe part in *The Asphalt Jungle.* I was too stupid to see the potential. I wanted to be the smart, wisecracking broad who second-guesses the detective. That was my role. That was what I played. Did you ever see me on the big screen, Lieutenant?"

"Yes, Ma'am. I remember you."

"Then you're no spring chicken, Columbo. What were you doing in life when you saw me?"

"I was a cop. That's what I've always been. I was a uniformed patrolman in New York, and Mrs. Columbo and I loved to go to the movies."

"Ahh . . . Twenty years ago, I'd have autographed a picture for you."

"I'd be honored to have one now, Ma'am."

"Well, quit calling me 'ma'am,' and I'll see if I can find one for you. Seriously . . . Faye was with us all evening. 'The girls.' We play bridge every Thursday. That's all we've got left, most of us."

"Ladies from the movie community," said Columbo.

"Not 'ladies,' Columbo. *Women.* Blanche Truman was a stunt rider. Tough as nails. Myrt Philips put makeup on the likes of Bette Davis and Joan Crawford. Eleanor Laurel was condemned by the Legion of Decency for being filmed in bed—not six feet away in her half of a twin bed, notice—with Tyrone Power."

"I remember Miss Laurel. She was one of the really big ones."

"Because she *had* really big ones."

Columbo smiled—not too broadly. "But Mrs. Wylie was never an actress. She—"

"Think not? She's been one *hell* of an actress all these years."

"Which means?"

"All these years she's pretended she was married to Dauntless Tim, the straight arrow. But she's not stupid, Lieutenant. Faye knew. She's always known."

"Known that he—?"

"If he'd been murdered twenty years ago, even ten maybe, I'd be telling you to go looking for the jealous husband or the outraged father."

"Sure is different from his image." Columbo shook his head. "I don't think I'll even tell Mrs. Columbo. She'd be awfully disillusioned. Y' know?"

"A lot of people would be disillusioned. Len's whole life was an illusion—a fraud, if you want to use the word."

" 'Course, what you're telling me gives Mrs. Wylie a motive for wanting him killed."

"So she hired somebody, you're suggesting? No way. If Faye had wanted him killed, she'd have had it done forty years ago. She sort of settled into comfortable acceptance of him and had no reason anymore."

"Jealous husband or outraged father," Columbo mused. "Well . . . Some people have long memories. Some people hold long grudges."

Letitia Coleridge frowned and smiled at the same time. "Are there things that bug you, Lieutenant Columbo? I mean, things that really make you uncomfortable, so much that you can't just leave them alone."

"Loose ends—"

"You got it! If you don't let me cut off that thread that's hanging from the bottom of your raincoat, it's going to drive me nuts! I've got a pair of scissors right here—"

He stared at the thread, six inches long. "Odd I didn't notice that. My wife makes a point of my not being neat enough. Which I guess I'm not."

The scissors had been within reach in her handbag, and she snipped off the thread. "Seeing that was like hearing chalk squeak."

"Well, I sure thank ya. I've gotta go."

"There's half a drink apiece left in the pitcher. A lonely

old woman doesn't very often get to talk with a homicide detective. Tell me, Lieutenant, how do you . . . ? *How?*"

"I just plug away at it, Ma'am— Excuse me, Miss Coleridge."

"Letitia!"

"Letitia. When I tell Mrs. C. I spent some time chatting with *you,* she's gonna say, 'Why couldn't *I* have been a cop? You get *all* the fun.' "

"But tell me something about how you solve cases."

"Uh . . . I just do it the only way I know how. I try to find out everything I can, then match all the facts to each other. I'm not a man who gets brilliant insights. I guess I'd have to say I do it reasonably well because I work hard at it. And I do that . . . uh, Letitia. I work hard at it."

She nodded. "That's the way I managed to act in films. I didn't have any talent. I just *worked* at it. That's how Len worked it, too. He had no particular talent. He just built a persona for himself and worked all his life at it. 'Course, he was fool enough to risk it constantly. Constantly. Faye could have shot him down anytime. So could a lot of others. I never understood why no one ever did. The bastard was *charming,* Lieutenant. He was charismatic. That's the word. Charismatic. *And* a fraud."

NINE

Saturday, April 15—9:08 A.M.

Sergeant Jesús Ruiz came to Columbo's desk just as he was pulling on his raincoat and leaving headquarters.

"Uh . . . it's not raining."

"Some guys carry briefcases. Me, I stuff all kinds of good things in my raincoat pockets. Cigars, matches, my notebook, a hard-boiled egg or two. And, speaking of matches, got one?"

Jesús handed over a lighter. He didn't smoke, but Sergeant Martha Zimmer had told him that if he was going to work with Columbo, he had better carry matches or a lighter.

"What's up, Jesús?"

"Well, you asked me to inquire around the neighborhood more, to see if anyone heard the shots." He shook his head. "No one did. But one of the neighbors had a few things to say about Wylie and his friends. You may want to talk to him."

" 'Bout what?"

" 'Bout what kind of guy he was. 'Bout who his friends were. He may give you a little different idea about what kind of guy Tim Wylie was."

"What's the name of this neighbor?"

"Victor Harris. This is his address."

9:51 A.M.

Columbo found Victor Harris riding around his lawn on a power mower. He was a man of seventy or so: trim, muscular, and vigorous, though deeply lined around his eyes and mouth and all but totally bald.

He glared for a moment at Columbo, then switched off the engine on his mower. "Who you?"

"Lieutenant Columbo, LAPD Homicide. Mrs. Harris let me in."

Harris climbed off the mower and extended his hand. "I guess Sergeant Ruiz did say you might stop by. What can I do for you, Lieutenant?"

Columbo raised his eyebrows and turned down the corners of his mouth. "Prob'ly nothin' much, Sir, and I'm sorry to be taking your time."

"How do you detectives say? 'Who got dead?' Well, Len got dead. I don't give a damn what you have to do to find out who did it, I want you to do it. I'm not one of those bleeding-heart liberals who worries about the 'rights' of murderers. I want the man who killed Len caught and locked up for the rest of his life."

"That's what I got in mind, Mr. Harris."

"Come over by the pool and sit down, Lieutenant

Columbo. At this hour a civilized man can have a drink, no matter what the goddamned doctors say. I'm going to have a light Scotch. Winston Churchill did, in the morning, and he lived into his nineties." Harris pressed a beeper he carried on his belt. "Summons the houseboy. Imagine that! Didn't have that sort of thing when we were boys, did we?"

"Sure didn't."

"Got any leads?"

"Well, Sir, I . . . Actually, Sir, I guess I have to say I really don't."

Harris sat down in a chair by the pool. "God, I hope Faye has an ironclad alibi. I promise you she didn't do it. I know you guys look at the spouses first, but—"

"Mrs. Wylie is not a suspect, Sir."

"Glad to hear it."

"Are you retired, Sir? Were you involved in the movie business?"

"I am retired. My sons run my business now. Our company creates special effects. One of our specialties is building models. Spaceships mostly, these days. In the past we did warships a lot. If you see a film where ships are firing at each other, damaging and sinking each other, you're likely looking at some of our work."

"You and Mr. and Mrs. Wylie were friends as well as neighbors?"

"Yes. Faye is a bit reclusive. She didn't invite people to the house much. Len did. He liked to sit down with a bunch of guys, watch a ball game on the tube, toss down a few. When he was younger he liked to organize a softball game—pickup teams, guys in the neighborhood and some friends. I can remember Jack Webb playing softball over there. Ralph Bellamy. Bill Holden. Steve McQueen. Lorne Greene. Len liked to do 'man' things. Except he wouldn't box. Some of the older guys did. Errol Flynn, for instance. But not Len."

Columbo nodded. "Interesting. Sergeant Ruiz says you didn't hear the shots."

"My wife and I would have been in the den on the other side of the house, watching television. Anyway, Lieutenant, I suppose you've heard the sound of a .32 Colt being fired."

"Can't say that I have."

"It's a sharp little crack, not a big bang. The sound would dissipate quickly in the structure of the house and in the distance between our two houses."

"Where did you hear one fired, Sir?"

"At a pistol range up in the mountains. I'm something of a collector. I have a Colt like that. I've fired it many times."

"Mr. Wylie had a gun collection, too, but he didn't have a .32 Colt."

"That's right, he didn't. If you were thinking he was maybe killed with his own gun, he wasn't—at least, he wasn't unless he had one I didn't know about. Some of us were interested in guns, you know, and we used to compare our guns."

Harris paused and grinned. "Lieutenant, I'm going to tell you something about Len. I liked the man. He was a friend, and I'm goddamned upset that he was murdered. But the unhappy fact is, Len was an awful fraud. He wasn't the cowboy he pretended to be. He hated horses. He was afraid of them. And he never fired that old .44 he always claimed was his favorite gun—not even blanks, not even once. You look at his films. You never see him actually fire that .44. He said the damned thing would make so much noise, it would damage his hearing."

Columbo frowned. "I'm sorry to have to ask you this,

Mr. Harris, but would you mind my taking your Colt into headquarters and letting the ballistics boys fire it into a box of sawdust?"

Harris stiffened and glared for a moment, then softened and smiled. "I didn't realize I was a suspect."

"You aren't. And the ballistics test will eliminate you absolutely. Won't it?"

The houseboy came with a bar cart. Columbo accepted a light Scotch and soda, and Harris sent the boy to bring out the Colt.

Harris told a story about Wylie bringing a girl home when Faye was in the hospital having a face-lift. "Hell, he invited me to come over and meet her. She was just eighteen, he said. She was drop-dead beautiful, and he was swelled up like the cat that swallowed the canary. He wanted to show her off and was sorry I was the only one he could call over to see her. He liked to talk about his amorous exploits. Some of the other guys did, too, but Len *gloried* in it. He was not a very nice guy in that respect, to tell you the truth. Faye put up with a lot."

The houseboy returned with the little automatic. It was not cocked or loaded. The clip was full of cartridges, but it was not in place in the pistol grip. Harris handed gun and clip to Columbo, who handled them gingerly. He put the pistol in one raincoat pocket, the clip in the other.

"I thank ya, Sir. I better not take any more of your time. I'll send your gun back as soon as it's fired—in an hour or so, I'd think."

"No hurry, Lieutenant. It's just a collector's item. I have no plans to fire it again soon."

Columbo stood. "I'll let you get back to your mowing. I guess I can go around the house and out to the driveway. Right?"

"Right."

Columbo walked toward the house. "I thank ya again for your time and the drink."

"Anytime, Lieutenant. And good luck."

"Thank— Oh, say." Columbo stopped and came back a few paces. "I guess I oughta ask about one other thing. Uh— Did Mr. Wylie ever mention Erika Björling?"

"No. I never heard him mention her name. I don't see how you guys can think *she* killed Len. Why would she do it?"

"Well, there's some evidence. I'm not free to discuss it yet."

"Somebody killed him so they could steal his art. Isn't that obvious?"

Columbo nodded. "I'd say that's the most logical explanation."

11:21 A.M.

Victoria Glassman lived in a Spanish-style house in Santa Monica, and Columbo drove out there. She had left a message for him: that what she had to tell and show him should not wait until Monday, that he should come and see it now. He'd called her and said he'd be there a little after eleven.

He rang the doorbell. A maid answered and ushered him into the living room, saying that Mrs. Glassman expected him.

Victoria Wylie Glassman was a different woman at home than she was with her mourning mother. She was casually dressed in faded blue jeans and a white T-shirt with no bra under it. She was barefoot, and she was smoking a cigarette. He glanced around her living room, trying not to be conspicuous about it. He knew that she was divorced from Glassman, who owned six automobile agencies in Southern California; and he guessed she received handsome alimony.

"Well, Lieutenant Columbo, I appreciate your coming."

"Glad to, Ma'am."

"Please don't call me 'ma'am.' You're not my servant."

"Habit of mine. I guess I picked it up when I was a beat cop in New York. I worked with a partner who was an older man, and he taught me a policeman always gets more respect when he offers respect."

"That's very admirable. But I doubt it works anymore. Not on the street, anyway."

"As a matter of fact, it does. A couple of weeks ago, I was lookin' into a murder on Florence Avenue. I went in a building, looking for a witness, and all of a sudden I'm facing a kid with a knife. I said to him, 'Sir, I'm Lieutenant Columbo, LAPD Homicide, and I'd appreciate it if you'd put that knife down.' And he did. I told him who I was lookin' for, and he told me where to find him."

"He probably figured if he didn't drop the knife you'd blast him. Uh . . . Would you have?"

"Well, no. I didn't have my gun with me."

"You went into that neighborhood without your pistol?"

"Didn't think it would help anything. Y' see, I'm not very good with it, and I figure I'll shoot myself in the foot. Or worse. Actually, I'm always afraid I'll miss a bad guy and hit somebody else."

"I thought you had to qualify on the police target range periodically."

"We do. But they issued me a new gun not so long ago, and I haven't quite got the hang of it yet."

She stared at him quizzically for a moment. "Okay, I asked you here because I have some things to tell you."

"In the first place, here's the album of photographs of the art Dad collected over the years."

"Oh. Thank ya." Columbo opened the album. "This is the van Gogh that—=?"

"Right. That's the van Gogh."

"Five million dollars. The man must have been some kind of artist. Mrs. Columbo would know something about that. She took some classes on art appreciation. I gotta do that, too. I really don't know enough about— Well . . . sorry. What else?"

She handed him a packet of letters, four of them, crudely typed on lined notebook paper. He read the first one.

You figure you got away with it, do you? Well, you didn't. I know it, and everybody knows it. You *stole* from me! I wrote that story, as you well know. You stole it and played like you owned it yourself. You didn't own it. You never owned it, you thieving son of a bitch. Figure on seeing me some night when you don't expect me. Nobody gets away with stealing from

JAY JOHNSON

"This Johnson character bugged Dad for years," Victoria said. "He was a screenwriter, one of those who got blacklisted in the McCarthy era. Even after the blacklist was dead, he couldn't get work. He kept submitting scripts. He sent them to studios, producers, directors, and actors. He sent Dad a script. Dad didn't even read it. You don't dare. What happened was *why* you don't dare. Johnson saw *Steel Weed* and decided it was the story he'd sent Dad— and that Dad had stolen the story. Hell, Lieutenant, something like four plots cover every western ever made, from Gene Autry to Clint Eastwood. But—"

"I can take these letters and—"

"Copy them. Use them. Whatever."

"He didn't kill my father," Victoria said quietly. "That poor old man is pitiful, not vicious."

"Yes, Ma'am."

"All right." She stopped and sighed. "Are you going to watch the Grant Kellogg news conference on television?"

"When?"

"Today. At one o'clock."

"Guess I'd better."

"He's going to make a public statement to the effect that Dad was the father of Erika Björling's daughter. He said you arrested Erika because you found a letter she wrote. You know what he did? He sent a messenger to Mother and to me, bringing us copies of the statement he's going to make and a pious little note, saying he didn't want us to be surprised and shocked to hear it first on television."

Columbo shrugged and scratched his head. "That letter's the best evidence we got."

"She accuses Dad of having kidnapped and killed Tammy." Victoria stopped and pressed fingers to her eyes, squeezing out tears. "Lieutenant . . . Dad was not a perfect husband to my mother and not a perfect father to me; but he was not capable of killing anyone, particularly not his own daughter."

"*Was* Tammy his daughter?"

Victoria nodded. "I didn't know. Mother called me when she got the statement from Kellogg. She told me. For fourteen years, Dad paid Erika $3,000 a month, child support. It was *extortion!* Blackmail. His reputation would have been ruined if the story had got out. He'd built his career on being an all-American hero. If it came out that he'd made a twenty-two-year-old girl pregnant— Well, there were times when he could hardly afford it. You know, his career went into eclipse for a while—when he was beyond the virile young stallion roles and not yet ready to do the grand old men with lined faces. It was hard for him to pay $36,000 a year."

"That'd be hard for anyone."

"Besides . . . Off the record, Lieutenant?"

Columbo nodded.

"Erika wasn't the only one. Even recently, he had to make some large payments. None as much as hers, but—"

"I guess I'll hafta watch the news conference. If I don't, I'll sure see it tonight. Mrs. Columbo will insist on having it on every time it's broadcast. Well . . . We were thinking about exhuming the body of—"

"Of my half sister," Victoria said bitterly.

"—and getting tissue samples so we could have DNA tests done to establish who the parents were. But if Erika says your father was—"

"I have something else to tell you, Lieutenant. I should have told you yesterday, but I thought maybe you'd catch the killer by now and it wouldn't be necessary. I'm still hesitant to say what I'm about to say, but— I guess I have to."

Columbo nodded. " 'Kay."

"My ex-husband pays me $15,000 a month alimony. The decree provides that when either or both of my parents die and I inherit something, his payments to me will be reduced by the amount I can make from prudent investment of my inheritance. Mel—that's his name, Melvin Glassman—thinks I'll inherit enough from my father to absolve him from all payments entirely. He's going to be surprised; I will not inherit nearly that much. As I've already told you, my father had to pay off some girls and parents."

"So what are you telling me?"

"That Mel might have done it, to save himself $180,000 a year. I don't know he did, but I can tell you he's the kind of man who's capable of it."

"I see. Well . . . you've given me a lot to think about. And I better be goin'."

"If you want to talk to my mother again on Monday, please call me, either here or at her house."

"I'll do that." He rose and moved toward the door. "I wanta thank you for your time. I know it's tough having to talk to a homicide cop at a time like this."

She got up and accompanied him into the hallway.

"You sure have an elegant place here. Well, I guess you grew up in an elegant place, what with all that beautiful art and all. And— Actually that raises a question, Mrs. Glassman."

"Call me Vicky, Lieutenant. Everyone does. I don't even think of myself as Mrs. Glassman anymore."

"Okay. Speaking of the beautiful paintings, something comes to mind. One of those little things, a sort of inconsistency that will stick in my mind till I figure out an answer. Uh— You say your father had some financial difficulties. I mean, you said it was difficult for him to pay the $36,000 a year?"

"Absolutely."

"But he had pictures on his walls worth— Well, they say four or five million for the one that's missing, and maybe that much more for the other two that were hanging beside it. How— How could he have been in financial trouble?"

Vicky shook her head. "I don't know exactly. I suppose it was because he couldn't bear to part with those paintings. I suppose also he'd have had horrible capital-gains taxes to pay. Of course, you know, he had them for many years. The prices weren't that high when he bought them. Art prices have gone out of sight in recent years."

"Oh, yeah. That prob'ly explains it. I thank ya. That would've bothered me if I couldn't come up with some explanation. I do thank ya."

TEN

1

Grant Kellogg made a point of being prompt, particularly when meeting with the news media. He knew that television stations would interrupt their programming to carry one of his news conferences, and it was only common courtesy to open a session when he had said he would. He had excellent rapport with the news media, which had often been of significant advantage to him, and this was one of the reasons.

Many lawyers and judges didn't like it, but public relations was an essential element of criminal defense—at least it was when you were defending a celebrity. The DA would go for his publicity. His problem was that he had no one on his staff with Grant Kellogg's skills for it.

He had summoned the media people to the Hyatt Wilshire Hotel, where he had rented a conference room. When he came into the room, more than fifty reporters were sitting on folding chairs facing the green-covered table where he would speak. Six television cameras pointed at the table. Eight microphones were clustered on the lectern. Some of the reporters had palm-sized tape recorders, which they held up and pointed toward him.

"Good morning, ladies and gentlemen," he said. "Thank you for coming."

He smiled warmly. This was what he did well, and he knew it. He was wearing a handsome gray double-breasted suit with a light-blue shirt and a regimental-stripe tie. He'd had his face lightly powdered just before he stepped out, so he wouldn't shine in the television lights.

"This morning I spent another hour and a half with Erika Björling, in the jail. I hardly need to tell you how difficult it is for her to find herself locked up and charged with murder, but she is bearing up well under her ordeal. She is a brave woman.

"We talked about the announcement that I am about to make to you. She and I agreed that what I am about to tell you should come from us, not from the DA or LAPD." He paused. "You will recall, I am sure, that Miss Björling suffered a horrible tragedy six years ago, when her daughter Tammy, who was fourteen, was kidnapped and murdered. Tim Wylie was the father of Tammy Björling. That is a fact to which I can attest, since I represented Miss Björling in negotiating an agreement for child support. There is no question about the matter. I have in my files his written acknowledgment that Tammy was his daughter."

Grant paused again. Some in the room gasped. Others began to chatter, as he'd known they would.

"In February, she thinks it was, Erika received an anonymous telephone call from a man who accused Tim Wylie of the kidnapping and murder of Tammy. He said he had helped Wylie dispose of the body, for which Wylie had paid him $10,000. I need hardly tell you that this call deeply distressed Miss Björling. The call seemed to make some sense, since the death of Tammy relieved Tim Wylie of an obligation to pay $36,000 a year, which obligation would have continued for another eleven years—that is, until Tammy was twenty-five—making the total cost to him over that eleven years almost $400,000. In any event, this telephone call temporarily disordered Miss Björling's mind, and she wrote a letter to Tim Wylie, accusing him of murdering their daughter and obliquely threatening him. It seems that Wylie kept that letter, and it was found by the police the night of his death. That appears to be the basis on which Miss Björling is charged."

Grant reached for a glass of water and took a sip.

"The fact that a work of art estimated as worth between four and five million dollars was stolen seems to have escaped the attention of the police." He stopped. "Perhaps I can answer a few questions."

"Does this suggest you may enter an insanity plea?"

"Absolutely not. Miss Björling did not kill Tim Wylie and will not enter any plea that admits she did. What is more, there will be no plea bargaining. We confidently expect her to be acquitted."

"What more can you tell us about her romantic relationship with Tim Wylie?"

Grant smiled. "She was twenty-two years old and just coming on as a television personality. He was a major motion-picture star with an international reputation. He was handsome, suave, experienced . . . Tammy was conceived in the living room of his home, while his wife was out playing bridge. He tried to duck responsibility, but Miss Björling retained me as her attorney, and we reached a satisfactory settlement."

A tall, thin woman stood and demanded his attention.

"Isn't it a fact, Mr. Kellogg, that you yourself once had an intimate relationship with Erika?"

He nodded. "Later. Briefly."

"Others?"

"I have no idea. But no matter how many, or who, that doesn't make her guilty of murder, does it, Miss Brinsley?"

2:11 P.M.

Sergeant Carol Davidson knew Columbo very well. She knew there was no point in leaving a memo on his desk saying she needed to see him. He avoided his desk as much as he could, and when he did visit it, he didn't read the accumulated directives and memoranda that made untidy piles.

To get his attention, you had to do something different. She had rolled her memo around a cigar and taped it.

Columbo grinned. "Aww . . . ," he said to no one in particular. "One of you guys a new father?"

He unrolled the memo and read it—

Got something interesting. Get to me when you can.

Carol

Her desk was in Crime Scene. He picked up two cups of coffee and went there. For once, he was not wearing his raincoat. It was draped over his chair.

"Hiya, kid. What's up?"

"Fingerprint report on the Erika Björling note to Tim Wylie. No prints. None. Nobody's. Not even Wylie's."

"Well . . . Paper. Not the best surface for fingerprints."

Carol Davidson would have liked milk and sugar in her coffee, but she picked up the black coffee he had brought and took a sip. For some reason, LAPD coffee was always the worst in town. Even the coroner's office did better. Actually, they even did better for the uniformed types. Something about detectives . . . "Not even smudges," she said.

Columbo frowned. "Now, that *is* a peculiar thing, isn't it?"

"I'd call it that."

Columbo sipped coffee. "I know you left on my desk a report about everything that Crime Scene found in the Wylie house. I also know you'd have made sure I read it if there was anything in it more than routine."

"Right. I know how you do business, Columbo."

He grinned. "Not by the book, exactly. I just can't discipline myself to have orderly habits. Anyway—"

"You're right that there was nothing that settles the case. Only Wylie's fingerprints on the glasses. And the alcohol concentration in the Scotch and bourbon does suggest that ice melted in the two drinks."

"Burglars . . . " Columbo shook his head. "Why would he have poured two drinks? And why didn't somebody drink them? Because he *knew* the person who killed him. He'd poured drinks, maybe for him and the murderer, maybe for two murderers, and was killed before anybody drank them."

"Is there anything else I can do for you?"

"Uh— The note was written with a ballpoint pen. I wonder if the lab can tell how long ago. I mean, does the chemical composition of ballpoint ink change over time? Mr. Kellogg, Miss Björling's lawyer, says she wrote the note two months ago. It'd be interesting—wouldn't it?—if the ink hadn't been on the paper more than a week."

"I'll ask."

"Thank ya. And next time for sure I'll remember your name."

"Will you also remember I like milk and sugar in my coffee?"

Columbo grinned. "Gotcha!"

3:08 P.M.

Grant Kellogg was alone in his office. Lila had worked until three o'clock, when he reminded her it was Saturday afternoon and sent her home. As she went out, he locked the door to be certain that no one would interrupt the telephone call he was about to make. Or overhear it.

He dialed an area code: 914. Harry Gottsman lived in Scarsdale, New York.

"Hello. Is Mr. Gottsman in? Grant Kellogg calling from Los Angeles."

He heard the woman remind her husband that they were going out to dinner and would have to leave the house in twenty minutes.

"Grant? Hey, have you got the *case!*"

"Haven't I just? Sorry I didn't get back to you earlier, but I'm up to my ass in alligators. I saw your gal at the news conference this morning."

"Front-page stuff, for sure."

"Great! Listen, Harry. You and I have always been able to talk in confidence, right?"

"Sure. Journalistic ethics, lawyers' ethics."

"Okay. I got a tip for you, but you must not disclose your source."

"I'm listening."

"About three miles from the Wylie house there's a motel called King's Court. The night desk clerk is a young fellow by the name of Dave Logan. He claims Erika checked into the place about seven o'clock on the night Wylie was killed and checked out, say, an hour and a half later. That, of course, would put her in the vicinity of the Wylie house at the pregnant hour. He'll be a witness for sure—and an important one, I figure. If you lay a little bread on him, I bet you can get an exclusive interview."

Harry Gottsman chuckled. "And of course a witness who's taken money for his story is a much less credible witness. Huh? Right?"

"You got it. I mean, it taints him so bad they may not be able to use him at all."

"Grant, if I ever get in trouble— Listen. What about an interview with Erika?"

"Jesus, Harry, I'm gonna have to auction that. But I'll get something for you. Count on it. If somebody else bids in an exclusive interview with her, I'll still have some hot background stuff for you. The way it goes these days, I figure television will bid highest. But— Well, it depends on who comes up with what."

"You wouldn't happen to have any pictures of her? I mean, topless or nude. I could pay a good price for those. The TV characters couldn't broadcast them, but I can publish them, for damned sure."

"I wouldn't be surprised if she's got some. She's a little inclined to modesty, but I'll ask her about them."

"I'll buy those. I'll pay top dollar. She's got to have some. She started out as a model, didn't she?"

"Let me see what I can come up with."

"Okay, Grant. For right now, I'll taint your witness for you. Keep in touch."

ELEVEN

1

Sunday, April 16—7:08 A.M.

One of Dog's pleasures was taking his master for a romp on the beach, especially early in the morning. It was then, when there were not many people around, that Dog earnestly tried to teach his master the fundamentals. He showed him how to chase gulls. He showed him how to grab flailing crabs and carry them in his teeth without getting nipped—usually. The technique of chasing at waves rolling in was a little more complex, since he had to judge them carefully and run at them, barking loudly, and retreating at precisely the right moment, lest the annoyed water overtake him and send him rolling up the sand. When it did, he had to show his master how to rid himself of salt water, capering up close so his master could see exactly how to shake.

All of this his master failed to appreciate. The man in the flapping raincoat, smoking the stub of a cigar, muddleheadedly watched while Dog ran industriously after gulls—and never ran after any himself. He never caught any crabs in his teeth. He stood back from the surf, as if he were afraid of the waves and didn't want to get wet. The problem was, he didn't pay attention. The best cavorting a dog could do did not distract the man from staring at young girls naked but for little strips of colorful cloth wrapped around them at odd places for some odd reason. Dog despaired of ever managing to teach his master anything.

As Columbo despaired of ever teaching Dog anything. He'd often said that Dog knew all he would ever know when he came to live with the Columbos—which maybe was all a dog needed to know. He knew how to drown his fleas in a neighbor's swimming pool. He knew how to scratch. He knew how to relax.

One thing about Dog— He lightened a man's spirits. But he did not distract his thoughts.

Columbo flipped away his cigar. He dipped in his raincoat pocket and pulled out a hard-boiled egg, which he peeled and began to eat. It would have been nice to have a little salt. It would have been nice to have a cup of coffee. But, then, a man couldn't have everything.

His thoughts moved from one thing to another—to Erika Björling's note and the inconsistency in her statement about when she left her apartment Thursday evening, also to the confident statement of the motel desk clerk that had seen her there, only a couple or three miles from the Wylie home, very near the time when Tim Wylie was shot. On the other hand, where was the van Gogh that was worth millions? And why did two other valuable paintings remain hanging?

Maybe he'd focused on the wrong inconsistencies and coincidences. Probably had. But that was the way these things went sometimes. One thing led to another, and all a man could do was follow. Sometimes it was as if the case solved itself, and all a detective had to do was go along.

"Say. What kind of a dog is that?"

He was drawn out of his brown study by the beautiful girl who was asking what kind of dog was Dog. Girls like her were the real reason his uncle had moved to California and then urged him to, years ago. A California beach girl: sun-bleached hair, a deep tan, a terry beach coat open and displaying her tiny red bikini.

"He's a basset hound, mostly."

"He looks like he's shrunk inside his skin."

"Wouldn't be surprised," Columbo said.

"What's he trying to do?"

"He's trying to chase the waves back. He knows I don't wanta get wet, so he tries to keep the tide from coming in. Never gives up. Oh, he takes good care of me. He thinks I want gulls, so he tries to catch some for me. Never catches any. On the other hand, two or three times he's brought me crabs. Or maybe *they* brought me *him*. I had to pry them loose off him."

The girl tilted her head and looked inquiringly at Columbo. "Haven't I seen you on television?"

"Afraid you may have."

"Yeah . . . Yeah! The Erika Björling case! You're, uh, Lieutenant . . . uh—"

"Columbo."

"Right! Hey! Did she really do it?"

Columbo lifted his eyebrows high and turned down the corners of his mouth. "Kinda looks like she did. It'll be for a court to decide."

"Well . . . Hey! Like, y' know, you and your dog are the most interesting people on the beach this morning."

"Uh . . . Well, uh . . . thank ya."

2

Columbo stood on the grass on a slope above the funeral chapel, in the shade of a pair of trees. Columbo had chosen today to wear a dark gray suit, and he'd left his raincoat in his car.

"Columbo . . ."

"Adrienne. I figured you'd be here. Famous reporter like you, you oughta be inside."

"I don't much care about being inside. I'd have to listen to the eulogies."

"You're gonna hear 'em out here," said Columbo. He nodded at the speakers mounted on the walls of the chapel.

Adrienne was dressed for a funeral: in a black dress, white gloves, and a little black hat with a veil that fell only over her forehead.

"Where's Dan?"

"Not over there," she said, noticing that Columbo was looking toward the hoard of cameramen and reporters jostling for position. "He's downtown. At the station."

"Writin' his report?"

She smiled. "Columbo . . . Dan doesn't write. He's not a reporter. He's an *anchor*. His job is to be pretty and sound good."

"He's both of those things, alright."

Adrienne squeezed Columbo's arm. "That's why I love him, I guess."

"Better reason than most," said Columbo.

She turned her attention to the limousines arriving at the

funeral chapel. "Everybody that's anybody. That's one thing Hollywood can still do: stage funerals."

The chauffeur-driven cars pulled up, one by one. People got out. Television cameras followed them as they walked into the chapel.

"Just like Academy Award night," said Adrienne.

"Except for the clothes."

No flamboyance. The death of Tim Wylie, even though it had been murder, had reminded many people of their mortality. The men especially looked pallid and genuinely depressed.

The hearse arrived. In recognition of Tim Wylie's military service, the coffin was wrapped in a flag, and it was carried by soldiers in dress uniform. Other soldiers, men and women, formed an honor guard that snapped to crisp orders.

When the coffin was inside, a limousine arrived carrying Faye Wylie, who was supported by her daughter as she walked slowly into the chapel.

"Why are you here?" Adrienne asked Columbo.

"You'd be surprised at how often a murderer shows up at his victim's funeral. It's worked out twice for me, other times for other detectives. You kinda look at the people standin' around, and you ask yourself why that person is there. 'Course, it doesn't work so well at a celebrity funeral."

Adrienne glanced around. "I recognize professional mourners. See that woman with the purple dress? She'll cry so hard she'll break down, and some kind souls will pick her up. Out of those kind souls she gets a drink or three—and sometimes even a dinner. When they carry the coffin out, she'll collapse. She'll tell people how well she knew him in the old days. They'll believe it. They'll tell their families and friends for years how they helped the woman who was Tim Wylie's first love."

"The average man or woman believes in the tooth fairy," said Columbo.

"Are you still convinced Erika Björling did it?"

"Between you and me, Adrienne—strictly between you and me—I'm *not* convinced. Evidence is pilin' up against her, but some way it's all too pat."

"The letter she wrote to Wylie is pretty tough evidence, isn't it?"

Columbo nodded.

"Seems like an odd thing for him to have left for two months in a drawer in the escritoire. Wouldn't you think he'd have wanted to hide it where his wife wouldn't find it? I'd think he'd have wanted to destroy it."

"It wasn't in the escritoire."

"The newspapers say it was."

Columbo shrugged. "I don't know where they get that idea. Prob'ly somebody guessed, and the rest of them fell in line."

"What about the van Gogh?"

"I got a set of high-quality photographs of the Wylie art collection. We're gonna ask the newspapers to run pictures of that painting, to see if anybody has seen it and wants to come forward."

"Columbo—"

"Huh?"

"I'd like to see that album. More than that, I'd like a man I know to see it. Have you ever heard of Professor Ted Chichak?"

"Can't say I have."

"Well, we're talking about the theft of a van Gogh. There's no greater authority in this country on Vincent van Gogh. I think it would be a good idea to let him see the photograph of the missing painting."

Columbo shrugged. "Why not?"

TWELVE

Monday, April 17—9:11 A.M.

Erika walked with her shoulders hunched forward. It was instinctive to walk that way when your hands were fastened at your waist with cuffs and a belly chain. Also she walked with an odd gait, toes pointed out. It was the first time she had ever tried to walk in leg irons, and she was afraid of jerking the chain and tripping.

Two of the other women on the bus walked the same way, for the same reasons. The other four ambled through the courthouse basement with no apparent concern. For them this was no new experience.

The guard separated Erika from the others, led her into a small room, and removed her chains. It was a dressing room, with a table and chairs and a mirror. In a shopping bag on the table were clothes for her appearance in court. Grant had gone to her apartment and taken them from her closet. He had brought her everything she had told him to bring, including a hairbrush and a tube of lipstick. She took off her blue dungarees, dressed in her own clothes—a black suit consisting of a knee-length skirt and a jacket over a white blouse—brushed out her hair, applied a modest amount of lipstick, and felt halfway human again.

Grant was waiting for her in the courtroom. Friendly but businesslike, as if there were no personal relationship between them, he took her hand and then pulled out a chair for her at counsel table.

"Good morning, most famous woman in America," he whispered.

"I wish I could give it up," she said. "I'd rather work topless."

"For four hundred a week? I'm already talking to a TV producer who's using figures like half a million for a jailhouse interview."

"I don't know if I can handle this."

"You *have* to handle it. Tim Wylie is dead."

"I had no idea what it would be like."

"It gets easier. The shock wears off. You settle into a routine. How many clients have I had who went through this? Fifty?"

"Couldn't you get me out on bail?"

"No. For two reasons. In the first place, they don't let people out who are charged with murder. More important, it would cost us big money. Public fascination and sympathy would diminish to half if you were out on bail."

She blinked out tears. "It's a horrible place, Grant. Full of horrible people."

"The judge—"

The bailiff rapped the gavel, and Judge Alicia Harding entered the courtroom and took the bench. She was a tall, thin woman with black hair. Erika thought she looked severe. Frightening.

"Good morning, counsel," the judge said with a perfunctory air, as if she expected the proceeding to bore her. "Good morning, Miss Björling." She nodded at the prosecution table. "Mr. Dunedin? Are you ready to proceed?"

Charles Dunedin rose: a somewhat pudgy young man in a three-piece blue suit. "The people are ready, Your Honor. The matter before the court is a simple case of aggravated murder. The people expect to prove that the defendant, Miss Erika Björling, shot and killed one Leonard DeMoll, popularly known as Tim Wylie. We are in possession of ample evidence to hold Miss Björling on the charge."

"Mr. Kellogg, is your client ready to enter a plea?"

Grant rose and motioned to Erika to stand beside him. "She is, Your Honor."

"Miss Björling, do you plead guilty or not guilty to the charge of murdering Leonard DeMoll, also known as Tim Wylie?"

Erika's voice caught in her throat, and it was only on her second try that she managed to murmur, "Not guilty."

"Mr. Kellogg, do you want a preliminary hearing on the question of whether or not the people have sufficient evidence to hold Miss Björling on this charge?"

Grant nodded to Erika to sit down again. "Your Honor, Miss Björling waives preliminary hearing. We also waive the grand jury and ask to proceed on information. We want to get the matter settled as expeditiously as possible, so Miss Björling may be released from jail. I do expect disclosure of their witnesses and other evidence, and we may have to hold hearings on issues that will arise about the evidence."

"The people will, I suppose, object to releasing the defendant on any sort of bond, pending trial?"

"Yes, Your Honor," said Dunedin.

"Miss Björling, you are remanded to the Sybil Brand Institute for Women pending trial. You are entitled to go to trial within one hundred twenty days. Since preliminary hearing is waived, the case will now be certified to the Superior Court."

The court recessed, and Erika was taken again to the dressing room to change back into her uniform. She was taken to a holding pen; the bus would not return prisoners to Sybil Brand until noon. There, for the first time, she was locked up with a dozen other prisoners.

"I hope you know how lucky you are, lady," said a glum black woman.

"Lucky?"

"To have a lawyer like you got. Me, I'm on my *way.* You, you're gonna *walk.*"

2

10:35 A.M.

Professor Ted Chichak was a sandy-haired man of medium build and the general appearance of a matured version of the Irish actor Kenneth Branagh. Columbo and Adrienne met him in his office on the UCLA campus.

The professor flipped through the dozen 8 x 10 color photographs in the album Columbo had picked up from Victoria Glassman. He shook his head. Then he laughed. "Ridiculous! Did no one artistically literate ever visit that house and view this collection?"

"Well, that wouldn't be me, Professor," said Columbo. "All I know about art is what kind of pictures I like. Why do you say 'ridiculous'?"

Professor Chichak regarded his two visitors for a moment, then said, "I tell you what. Let's take a little drive out to the Getty Museum. I don't want you to have to rely on just my opinion. I'll let you see the *facts.*"

In the parking lot, the professor stared for a moment at Columbo's Peugeot. "Why don't I drive? I know the way."

In the Getty Museum, he led them directly to the gallery he had in mind. He pointed at a painting on the wall, then at a photograph in the album.

"Henri de Toulouse-Lautrec, *'Entrer en danse.'* On loan from the Museum of Modern Art in New York. The painting. The photograph. Identical, hey? Only not identical. The painting is authentic. The photograph is a picture of a fake!"

Adrienne drew a deep breath. "Maybe Toulouse-Lautrec did more than one 'Entering the dance' in this style."

"Yes. And maybe van Gogh did more than one *'Printemps du verger.'* And maybe Picasso did more than one *'Harlequins nus.'* And here's a picture of what purports to be a Rouault. Maybe all these artists did other paintings that could bear these titles. Only they didn't. Picasso did many *saltimbanques,* nude and clothed. But all of them varied. This one is identical to the one that hangs in the Picasso Museum in Paris. The *'Printemps du verger.'* is in the Tate Gallery in London." Professor Chichak slapped the album. "There are one or two pictures in here I can't identify immediately, as to where the genuine paintings are; but I can tell you for a certainty: the entire collection is a fake!"

"Millions of dollars. . . ," Columbo muttered.

The professor handed the album to Adrienne. "The entire collection shown in these photographs is not worth ten thousand." He shrugged. "Competent fakes are worth something. A thousand each is not an unreasonable number." He reached for the album and opened it again. "Some of these are not even *good* fakes. My God! Didn't *anyone* ever *look* at these paintings?"

Adrienne grinned. "There are highly educated people in the film industry," she said. "Apparently, none of them came to the Wylie house. Or maybe those who saw his fakes were too polite to tell him. Obviously, *he* didn't know."

Columbo shook his head. "I'm afraid that's not the way of it. He didn't insure them. He didn't want appraisers to see them. He—"

"In this as in much else," said Adrienne, "the late Tim Wylie was a fraud."

12:47 P.M.

Columbo took the elevator to the fourth floor of the building on Sixth Street. At least there was an elevator, even if its floor was littered with cigarette butts and it was slow and rattly. He pressed the button of apartment 4B, but heard no buzz or ring inside, so he rapped on the door.

The man who opened the door and stared at him through thick little eyeglasses was hunched and slight and apparently eighty years old or more. He was dressed in a white T-shirt and a pair of khaki slacks.

"Mr. Johnson? I'm Lieutenant Columbo, LAPD Homicide."

"You took your time about coming. You expect me to stay home and wait for you? Good thing for you I've finished my lunch. I wouldn't see you during my lunch."

The old man stepped back from the door and tilted his head to invite Columbo into a small, littered apartment. The living room was dominated by a huge round coffee table covered with the tools of a writer: a huge old Underwood manual typewriter, two reams of typing paper, an untidy stack of typescript, a jar of pencils, pens, and type-writer erasers, and a big round brown ashtray almost full of cigarette butts.

Jay Johnson sat down behind all this, on a frayed old couch, and plucked a short-but-still-burning butt of a cig-arette from the ashtray.

"I'm sorry to bother you, Mr. Johnson."

"The hell you are. Anyway, you're not bothering me. All you have against me are those letters I wrote to the son of a bitch, and you'll never convict me of murder on those. Sit down. That chair over there won't damage your back-side."

"You're not a very good suspect, Sir. That's why I didn't come sooner."

"Not a very good suspect? Oh, hell. I was hoping you'd arrest me, handcuff me, take me in and lodge me in jail, then grill me. That kind of thing holds no terror for me. I went through it before, you know, forty years ago."

"Contempt of Congress," said Columbo.

"Right. These days everybody holds Congress in con-tempt, but I went to jail for it. Worse than that, I was de-prived of my means of earning a living. Blacklisted. This script right here in the typewriter will be seen by tens of millions of people on television, but the screen credit will list another writer. My name is still poison."

Jay Johnson drew hard on his cigarette and burned away all that remained of it. He dropped it in the ashtray.

"You wrote some threatening letters to Mr. Wylie."

"He stole a story of mine, that's why. He was a mil-lionaire many times over, I live here in squalor, and *he* steals from *me!* Well . . . What else is new? The rich steal from the poor. That's how they get rich."

"Did you know the man at all?"

"Len? Sure I knew him. He was a liar and a fraud."

Columbo pulled a cigar from his raincoat pocket. "Gotta match?" Johnson handed him a book of paper matches, and Columbo lit the cigar. " 'Liar and fraud.' I keep hearin' that. Well— I better be goin'. I'm sorry to interrupt your work."

"I wish more people did."

"You're not a suspect, Mr. Johnson."

"Oh. I'm disappointed. It might have been fun, for a while."

Columbo stood. But he paused, frowning, and did not move toward the door. "Did you know Mr. Wylie in the days before you were blacklisted?"

Johnson nodded. "Lieutenant! You wanta know? You really wanta know?" He shook out a cigarette—an unfiltered Camel—and lit it. "You wanta take the time to hear? I'm gonna have a shot of gin. You?"

"I'm on duty, Sir."

Pouring a shot of gin was only a matter of reaching for a bottle and a glass. Johnson didn't worry about ice. "You know how long I been around Hollywood? I sold my first script to MGM in 1936. By the time Leonard DeMoll— Tim Wylie—showed up, in 1939, I was one of the hottest properties in town—hotter than he was. I didn't meet him until 1941, when he had a supporting role in a picture I wrote. But we got to know each other. Drinking buddies. He was married to Faye, but he already— Well, you've heard. Nobody can ever take his war service away from him. He did his duty, and maybe more. When he came back in '46, he thought he was going to play war heroes, like Audie Murphy, like some other guys." Johnson shook his head. "*I* was the guy that told him to try westerns. 'Ha!' he says. 'Oaters? Not this guy.' But he did it, and I wrote his best parts. When I got in trouble, he didn't know me. That was Len. That was Tim Wylie. Orson Welles still knew me. Spence Tracy still knew me. But—" He shook his head. "Len didn't know me. The son of a bitch *testified* he didn't know me!"

"Sir— Do you know anything about the murder?"

Johnson nodded. "I know there are a hundred guys in town, and fifty women, who are glad he's dead."

"Do you know Faye Wylie and Victoria Wylie Glassman?"

"Lieutenant! Don't you know *anything?* In all the years she was stuck in that awful marriage, Faye stepped out of it only one time. do you know with who?"

"Who, Mr. Johnson?"

"With me, for Christ's sake! I wasn't always an eighty-year-old schmuck."

"And—?"

"What do you think? Me, a blacklisted writer, out of jail but living like . . . this. She loved me. I'm sure she did. But to give up what she had— No way."

"Erika Björling? Whatta ya know about her?"

"I know that poor, pitiful child didn't kill Len. Yeah, I saw the news story—she thinks Len maybe killed Tammy. But I can tell you two things: One, Len didn't kill his daughter. That cowardly son of a bitch couldn't have killed a burglar. Second, poor little Erika couldn't have killed Len." Johnson shook his head. "Y' wanta know something, Lieutenant? Faye knew about Erika. *And* Tammy. She felt sorry for them both."

"What do you know about his art collection?"

"Only what Faye told me. Fakes. Nothing but fakes. Len was a fake; his collection was fakes. Okay?"

THIRTEEN

1

Monday, April 17—2:13 P.M.

Columbo paused to tighten the knot of his necktie before he rang the bell at the door on North Perugia Way. He glanced down and shook his head. The little end hung below the wide end. Tied carelessly again. Well, he'd rung the bell and could not pull his tie loose now. Anyway, it didn't have any cue chalk on it, or any chili.

Victoria Wylie Glassman answered the ring. "You're prompt, Lieutenant," she said crisply. "Thanks. Mother and I are out by the pool again this afternoon."

Faye, who the other day had sat in a chaise lounge in a blue bathrobe, today sat in a white terry beach coat, showing her tanned legs. Victoria wore an almost-identical short coat, open and showing an iridescent-blue bikini.

Without asking if he wanted it or not, Vicky poured Columbo a vodka gimlet. She pushed toward him on the glass-topped table a platter of lox and cream cheese, with crackers, no bagels. "The Department will forgive you."

"I'm sure it will, Ma'am."

"C'mon, now. Call me Vicky."

Columbo spoke to Faye. "Something is gonna be in the papers, Ma'am. I thought I'd better stop by and tell you before you read it. Y' see, the fact is, the van Gogh painting that was stolen is a fake. So are all the other paintings in the collection—according to a professor of art at UCLA who looked at the photographs."

"How could he tell from photographs?" Vicky asked sharply.

"The van Gogh painting hangs in an art gallery in London. The Toulouse-Lautrec picture is out at the Getty Museum. I saw it this morning. It's exactly the same as the one hanging in the living room here."

"You mean, Dad was—"

"Defrauded?" Faye interrupted. She shook her head. "No. He knew they were copies. Millions of dollars' worth of art? Len never *had* millions."

"We're making some effort to find out where he bought them, Ma'am."

"What's the difference? He had them for twenty years and more. The forger is probably dead. He probably bought all of them from the same forger. Not a very good forger, I guess, since your professor saw through them so easily."

"It was just because he knew where the real paintings are."

"I wonder how many of our friends they fooled all these years—and how many just smiled behind their hands and concluded Len and I were either dupes or liars."

Columbo sipped from the gimlet. He wasn't sure if it had alcohol in it or not but guessed it did. He took a piece of the lox. He loved all kinds of seafood, and he recognized this cured salmon as expensive and tasty.

"Liars, is what they had to think," Faye went on. "I'd

rather be thought that than a fool. Len was a fraud. In everything he did. A fraud. And a lecher nonpareil."

"Mother!"

"Face it, Vicky. Your father was a satyr."

Faye shrugged. "Lieutenant Columbo, my husband would have mounted a sheep or a goat if he hadn't had a woman during the past twenty-four hours. I mean, he would have when he was younger. I'm not sure how long ago *that* ceased to be a possibility. He enjoyed himself with most of the actresses and wannabe actresses during the fifty years he was a star. Most of them thought they were honored."

"He sure didn't have that reputation, Ma'am."

"Everyone in the business has, I should imagine, *some* talent—the great ones like Bette Davis and Katharine Hepburn and Spencer Tracy and Jimmy Stewart and Humphrey Bogart had *real* talent; others like Clark Gable and John Wayne and Rock Hudson had a talent for pleasing the public while cleverly hiding the fact that they didn't have talent shit—"

"Mother—"

Faye went on. "Joan Crawford had talent enough to conceal the fact that she broke into show business as a star of stag films. Marilyn Monroe broke out of the ranks of starlets because she was willing to French any producer who asked her. Jimmy Dean had no talent whatever for anything, except for scowling and pretending he was—"

"Mother . . . Lieutenant Columbo doesn't need a history of Hollywood."

"My husband had a lifelong ambition: to be like Henry Fonda. To achieve what Fonda did. To be honored by people who really knew talent from popularity."

"Mother—"

Tears streamed down Faye's cheeks. "Look for an aggrieved husband, Lieutenant.

"Can you name names, Ma'am?"

"Eva Cline," Victoria said glumly. "Her husband divorced her because of Dad."

Faye sobbed. "Try for a father, Lieutenant Columbo. In recent years, he developed a predilection for *girls*. The younger the better."

"How'd he keep all this stuff secret?" Columbo asked.

"He paid people off," said Faye. "He'd have left a bigger estate if— Well. Besides, there's a conspiracy in the media to preserve certain names. His was one of them. Even tabloid TV wouldn't touch him."

"Any other women? Girls?"

"Lots of others. Oh, yes, others. We'll think of others. We'll make a list."

Columbo rose. "It's kind of disillusioning," he said.

"My husband made a career of illusion."

"Well, thank ya. I'll be going. Maybe some of these leads will— Oh. Say. One more thing. Miss Björling's lawyer says she wrote the note to Mr. Wylie two months ago. Did he ever mention receiving a note from Miss Björling?"

"No," said Faye.

"*Would* he have? Was it like him to keep secret a note accusing him of murdering his daughter?"

Faye shook her head. "I don't know. In spite of everything, he did confide in me, generally. That's how I know about the girls he— Maybe he would have told me if he had received a threatening letter."

2

4:24 P.M.

"Hey, Columbo!"

Striding through the hall, raincoat flapping around him,

Columbo stopped, turned, and faced Captain Sczciegel. "What can I do for you, Captain?"

"Apart from carrying your sidearm in compliance with official regulations, you can explain how this newspaper story got loose."

The captain was a tall man who was all but totally bald and chose to shave off á la Kojak the little gray hair that remained to him. He brandished a folded newspaper as though it were a weapon.

"Haven't see a newspaper story. What paper is that, Captain?"

"Only this week's *PROBE*. Looka this—"

ERIKA WAS THERE, WITNESS SAYS! CHECKED IN AND OUT OF MOTEL ROOM IN WYLIE NEIGHBORHOOD
Special to *PROBE*
by Betsy Mahoney

The desk clerk at a motel less than three miles from the Bel Air estate where Hollywood star Tim Wylie was murdered last Thursday says that Erika Björling, former star of the long-popular TV game show *Try It Once* checked into his motel about 7:00 p.m. and checked out less than two hours later.

The busty, long-legged sex goddess, who was the source of the game show's long run, has been charged in the murder and now languishes in jail.

David Logan says he recognized the star from the moment she checked in and paid cash for her room—even though she registered under a false name.

"Tough talk," said Columbo. "Y' gotta like the picture, though." He pointed at a photograph of Erika Björling posing in a brief bikini. "This case gets more and more difficult."

"Why you figure this Logan character gave the interview?" Sczciegel asked.

"The paper paid him money."

"Right. Which means jurors won't believe him. The question is, who told the reporter that—"

"Aw now, Captain. I know you're not suggestin' *I* did. How long's a man gotta serve before—?"

"No, Columbo. I know you didn't tell. What I wanta know is, you got any idea who did?"

Columbo shook his head. "Had to be Dave Logan himself. Which makes his testimony completely worthless. If he sold his story—"

"The DA is going ballistic," Sczciegel said. "It was a break to have a witness that put Erika Björling near the scene of the crime at the right time. Now—" He shrugged. "Pfft."

"I can go talk to Logan."

"An assistant DA is doing that."

"Captain, we gotta consider that Miss Björling may not be the right one."

"She did it, Columbo. Concentrate on her."

4:38 P.M.

On his desk he found a cigar wrapped in a note. Okay. Carol Davidson wanted to see him. He picked up coffee, put milk and sugar in it, and went to her office.

"It pays to work with a genius," she said.

"Just 'cause I remembered how you like your coffee doesn't make me a genius."

She grinned, but she shook her head. "Saturday you asked me to have the lab test the ballpoint ink on Erika Björling's letter to Wylie. Bingo! Grant Kellogg says she wrote the letter in February. The lab says that oxidation of the ink has not proceeded beyond a week."

Columbo scratched his ear. "Wonder what's the explanation for that. Somebody's not tellin' us the truth, I don't think."

FOURTEEN

1

Adrienne Boswell sat at a table in a restaurant called Emilio's. She frowned over a newspaper clipping and sipped from a martini on the rocks. She was waiting for Columbo, and he was a few minutes late.

"Sorry," was his first word. He shrugged out of his raincoat and hung it over a chair. "Hey, you sure do look elegant today!"

"Thank you, Columbo." She was wearing an emerald-green jacket and miniskirt over a pale-yellow knit shirt. "Martini?"

"Uh, well, I'm on duty, but I guess a Scotch and soda would be okay."

Adrienne signaled their waitress and told her to bring another martini for herself and a Scotch and soda for Columbo.

"I'm sorry I'm late. I had a meeting with the assistant DA this morning. Mr. Kellogg is pressing for an early trial of the Erika Björling case. So far as I'm concerned, we're not ready yet. I'd like to see some more evidence."

"Off the record, you don't think she did it, do you?"

"Well . . . she prob'ly did."

"You've seen the *PROBE* story, I assume. And have you seen this?"

She handed him the clipping she had been reading. It was from yesterday's—Monday's—edition of the *Sun*. Adrienne had clipped Peg Brinsley's column. Part of it read:

For years a conspiracy of silence has kept secret the intimate escapades of the late Leonard DeMoll, better known as Tim Wylie. His violent death may serve at long last to correct the record on a man who was one of Tinseltown's most aggressive skirt-chasers.

It is known in Hollywood but studiously kept from public knowledge that "Tim Wylie" was the man behind the scandalous divorce of sex symbol Eva Cline. Wylie, then in his sixties, bedded the gorgeous Eva, then in her twenties, and outraged her husband, Victor. Why did the name of Eva's paramour not come out? Two reasons. Eva did not contest the divorce, and . . . $$$.

The same "reasons" quieted what could have been a far more serious matter, the affair between sixty-something Tim and sixteen-or-so Natalie Moore.

Erika Björling was not the only person in town with a motive to murder the sexagenarian Lothario.

Columbo sighed and shook his head. "Jeez," he said. "I sure hope Mrs. Columbo doesn't read this. She will, though. She reads all this kinda stuff. Keeps me filled in on it."

"Did you read my story about the art?"

"I sure did. Those two women who wrote those stories aren't in your class, Adrienne."

"Thank you. There aren't many detectives in your league, Columbo."

"Aw, a lot of fellas outclass me."

They paused while the waitress put their drinks on the table.

"I've been looking around a little," Adrienne said. "I've got some news for you."

"I'll appreciate it."

"Grant Kellogg has hired an agent."

"Meanin'?"

"He's getting ready to peddle the rights to some story. And it has to be the Erika Björling story."

"But the case isn't even—"

"He's getting ready. He hired the Murray Hill Agency in New York."

"Because—?"

"Because there's millions of dollars to be made. Every newspaper, magazine, and broadcast station in the country is slavering over this story. The death of Tim Wylie and the arrest of Erika Björling are *big business,* Columbo. Don't you know that?"

"Well, I try to keep outa that side of things."

"Columbo, publicity may be the key to this case."

He grimaced and rubbed his right ear. "I guess I'll have to go see this Peg Brinsley. What can you tell me about her?"

Adrienne shrugged. "She's a onetime actress. She has to be, oh, fifty years old. She played ingenue roles in the sixties—in beach films and stuff like that, nothing challenging. She grew out of that kind of thing and found nothing else waiting for her. Before she was thirty she was unemployed but was still something of a Hollywood figure, known around the town. So she exploited her connections and a talent for snooping and writing and managed to syndicate a newspaper column. It was once syndicated in ninety-five newspapers but appears in thirty-two now—and only three times weekly. She has always skirted just around the boundaries of the libel laws. In fact, she's been sued a number of times. She has a following, though. Some people wouldn't miss her column. I suppose millions of people."

"I guess I'll have to go see her," Columbo said unhappily.

"Well, let me give you one or two more facts about her. She's had her face lifted. And when she was in her twenties, she suffered some kind of fever and lost her hair. Under the wig you'll see her wearing, she's bald as a cue ball."

5:00 P.M.

Peg Brinsley received Columbo at her Malibu apartment. He was careful to be on time, at the exact hour she had specified.

She was not wearing a wig and was as bald as Adrienne had said.

"I'll talk about my head once, Lieutenant, and then—"

"Oh, you don't have to do that, Ma'am. That's none of my business."

"Lieutenant. I wear wigs when I go out, so as not to be a public spectacle. I do not wear them in the privacy of my home. They are not very comfortable. So . . . Don't try to keep your eyes off my bald head. Stare all you want to. I have long since ceased to be embarrassed."

"In point of fact, Ma'am, it's sort of distinguishing, if you don't mind my sayin' so."

She laughed. "Come into my living room, Lieutenant. Take off your coat and have a seat. I invited you for the cocktail hour, so what will you have?"

"A light Scotch and soda, Ma'am."

She kept a bar in her living room, complete with a small refrigerator and a score of bottles. He watched her pour his Scotch and a Stolichnaya vodka on the rocks for herself. A silver platter of cheeses and crackers sat on the coffee table.

Columbo decided Adrienne's description of Peg Brinsley had been catty and wondered if it were not based on professional jealousy of the woman's following. He stared at her as she had invited him to and decided her baldness did not detract from the simple truth that she was a handsome woman. Perhaps her face had been smoothed by a plastic surgeon; he was no judge of things like that, seeing only that her features were firm and smooth. She had blue eyes and probably had been a blond. He guessed she paid regular visits to a manicurist and a cosmetician. Her figure was one any man could admire. She was wearing powder-blue silk lounging pajamas. When she brought their drinks and sat down, she opened a lacquered box on the coffee table and took out a pale-green oval cigarette.

"Care to try one of these?" she asked.

"Well, no Ma'am, but since you smoke, maybe you won't mind if I smoke a cigar."

"Not at all."

He felt that a gentleman should light a lady's cigarette and was glad to see a lighter on the table.

"What can I do for you, Lieutenant?"

"Well, Ma'am, I could use some more details on those two names you mentioned in your column about Tim Wylie."

"I can't disclose my sources."

"Oh, I understand that. I wouldn't ask ya to. But it would be helpful to me if you could tell me some facts, like where does Natalie Moore live and when did this happen—stuff like that."

"I can give you the addresses and phone numbers of the Moore home and Moore's business. When did it happen? About a year ago. Natalie was sixteen. Len was almost seventy. I ask you, Lieutenant Columbo, is that grotesque, or is that not grotesque?"

"I try not to be judgmental, Ma'am, but yeah, I gotta admit, that's grotesque. Why weren't the juvenile authorities called in?"

"Len paid off."

"In the case of Eva Cline, I guess I know where I can find her."

"She's shooting a picture right now."

"In your column you mentioned motives to murder . . . uh, Tim Wylie."

"Eva's husband threatened to kill him—threatened him personally, to his face. Arnold Moore threatened him on the phone."

Columbo reached for his raincoat, and Peg Brinsley's eyes widened as she watched him pull a half-smoked cigar out of a pocket and light it with her table lighter.

"I know ya can't disclose your sources, but can you say you're really sure about these threats?"

"Arnold Moore called me and asked me to blow the whistle on Len. He said he'd threatened to kill him but guessed maybe public exposure of his lechery would hurt him more. He offered an interview with his daughter, and photos of her. The next day he called me again and said he'd decided not to go through with it. He asked me to forget it. I asked him point-blank how much he'd been paid. He said nothing, but he wasn't convincing."

"And Eva Cline's husband?"

"He threatened Len in public, at a party. He had to be restrained from punching him in the mouth. Plenty of witnesses to that."

"You mentioned a conspiracy of silence about Mr. Wylie's activities."

"Lieutenant . . . Some people become icons. No matter how aggressive news people get, they leave some people alone. That's true in politics. For example, do you read enough tabloid stuff to know that Marybeth Lane had an illegitimate child last month?"

Columbo shook his head. "I don't pay much attention to that kinda stuff. Mrs. Columbo does. She likes the scandal shows, but me——"

"The name of her child's father has not been made public. A lot of people in the news business know who it is, but they're not publishing or broadcasting it. Why not? Because the not-so-proud papa is United States Senator Alexander Douglas. An icon. Nobody wants to bring him down. You see, there is some restraint in the media."

"And Tim Wylie——"

"Was an icon."

"Until now. You decided to——"

"I had to fight to get the column published. Eleven of my newspapers refused to publish it. I've had angry phone calls, even on my unlisted number. Telegrams. Faxes. How could I do this to the idol of millions?"

"You've known all this stuff for years, Ma'am. Why did you decide to do it now?"

"I tried for years to do it. My syndicate wouldn't run anything negative about Tim Wylie."

"You tried . . . because?"

Peg Brinsley tossed her head and laughed. "Can't you guess? I was one of his victims. For about three weeks. My bald head turned him on. He said he loved me. He said he'd divorce Faye and marry me. Then, as suddenly as he 'fell in love,' he fell out of it. Off he went, with somebody else. You know how I felt? I felt *dirty*, Lieutenant. He—" She stopped and ran a hand over her smooth head. "This—" Her voice broke. "This was what he wanted. For the moment. And once he'd experienced making love with a bald woman . . . What turned him on turned him off."

"I'm sorry, Ma'am."

"Drink up, Lieutenant. 'Eat, drink, and be merry, for tomorrow ye die.' "

"I've heard that said, Ma'am."

"Let me pour you another one."

"Actually, I've gotta be goin'. You know, constabulary's duty's to be done."

"And your wife is preparing a nice dinner."

He grinned and shook his head. "Lasagna. It's one of her specialties."

"You live an enviable life."

"Thank ya, Ma'am. I think I do."

Peg Brinsley nodded. "You go home and enjoy your nice dinner."

He rose and picked up his raincoat. "I sure do appreciate your help."

"Anytime, Lieutenant," she said warmly. She followed him to the foyer and opened the door. "Anytime."

He stepped into the hall and pressed the elevator button. Then—

"Oh. Oh, say, Ma'am. There is one more little thing I meant to ask. Uh . . . You comin' up with these ideas about how other people had a motive to murder Tim Wylie, that's a good thing for Miss Björling's defense, wouldn't ya say?"

"I would think so."

"Right. And your column appeared yesterday. So has

Mr. Kellogg called you to get more facts, like I've just done?"

Peg Brinsley tilted her head and smiled. "As a matter of fact, no. He hasn't. Which is curious, isn't it? I wondered if you'd ask. You're damned sharp, Lieutenant Columbo."

"Not really, but— That's interestin' . . . Well, maybe he just hasn't got around to it. Would you call me if he does?"

"I'll call you. I'll make a point of calling you."

"I'll be grateful, Ma'am."

FIFTEEN

Wednesday, April 19—8:22 A.M.

The AAA tow truck sat in Columbo's driveway, just behind his Peugeot. The driver, in white coveralls, shook his head and grinned at the same time.

"Mister, the only thing I know to do is hook onto this car and drag it to a Peugeot dealership—and I'm not sure there's one of those in Los Angeles. I'll have to call in and check. I guess there's a Saab dealer who services—"

Columbo shook his head. He pulled his cigar from his mouth. "Naa," he said. "Y' don't need to tow it in. I know what's wrong with it and how to fix it, but I haven't got the tools. I've seen it done ten times, and I can show you how. Just get out your metric socket wrenches." He jammed the cigar back in and drew a mouthful of smoke, which he blew away in the wind.

The tow-truck driver sighed. "Mister, I ain't got—"

"Hey! I don't mean to throw weight around or nothin', but I'm a police officer, and I've gotta get down to—"

"You're a police officer?"

"Lieutenant Columbo. Homicide. I'm workin' on the Tim Wylie murder, and—"

"I saw you on TV!"

"Yeah, yeah. May have. Look. Y' see this thingamajig?"

"That's the carburetor, Lieutenant."

"Right. That's what they call that. Now, you see that thing there? I can't turn that with pliers, 'cause it's down there in that little slot. You gotta use a socket wrench."

"And do what?"

"And turn it. I'll tell you when it's enough."

The driver went to his truck and returned with a kit of tools. He bent over the fender of the Peugeot and tried sockets until he found one that fit.

"I always admire good tools and guys who know how to use 'em," Columbo said. "My wife is always tellin' me I ought to buy a set of those wrenches so I could do this for myself. But I tell ya. The last time I tried to fix anything mechanical, I lost a screw down inside an electric motor. When I plugged it in again, that screw chewed up that motor somethin' awful. Mechanical things just defy me."

"How you want me to turn this?"

"Right. Right about a quarter of a turn. Y' see, what happens is, in time vibration shakes that whatchamacallit loose, and it turns and— What ya want to do is tighten it. Just snug. One guy broke it off one day. Just snug."

"It needs a locknut, Lieutenant."

"Yeah, prob'ly. You wouldn't happen to have one of those in your toolbox?"

"Not that'll fit this."

"Okay. That's enough. It'll start now."

"You sure?"

"Absolutely. It'll start."

"You wanta try it?"

Columbo shrugged. "Why not?" He sat down behind the wheel, engaged the starter, and the engine sputtered to life. He turned it off and got out again. "Y' see? It's just—"

The driver shook his head. "What I don't understand is why you try to keep an antique like this runnin'."

"Well . . . Y' gotta understand. Y' see, this car's a French car, and the French really know how to make a car—or did when they made this one. You wouldn't believe how many miles— I don't even *know* how many miles it's got on it. And it's got lotsa good miles left in it. When ya got something good, you take care of it, and—"

"If I were you, Lieutenant, I'd take out my service revolver and shoot it, like a horse that's—"

"Well, I can't do that."

"Y' can't?"

"No. Y' see, they took away our good old service revolvers and issued us these automatics. I can't figure out how to load and cock the thing, let alone not shoot myself in the foot. Anyway, I couldn't shoot a good ol' horse that had given me faithful service. If this car ever gets where it can't start anymore, I guess I'll just leave it in the garage, and I'll go out and sit in it and talk to it once in a while."

10:11 A.M.

Eva Cline swam toward the beach. A following wave caught her, lifted her, and threw her tumbling onto the sand. She scrambled to her feet and ran up the beach. She was naked.

"Right! Good! Perfect!"

A girl ran up to Eva and helped her to cover herself with a thick, ankle-length, terry-cloth robe. The electrician turned off the lights. The cameramen checked their cameras to be sure they'd gotten the scene. The director clapped his hands and kept yelling how good it had been.

"Eva! Eva! One cut. That's it. We don't have to do it again!"

"Thank God for something anyway," she said. "A girl could drown."

"Never! Twenty-one guys would have been into the surf to save you! Oh, uh . . . this is Lieutenant Columbo of the Los Angeles Police. He, uh, wants to talk to you."

She grinned at Columbo. "Indecent exposure?" she asked playfully.

"Nothin' indecent about it, Ma'am. No. I'm from the Homicide Squad. If you don't mind, I'd like to ask you a question or six."

"Well, come on to my trailer, Lieutenant. Homicide . . . Sounds ominous. Who'm I supposed to have killed?"

"I'm working on the Tim Wylie case."

"Oh . . . Poor Len."

Eva Cline was a handsome woman who could not escape the adjective "statuesque." She had light-brown hair, hazel eyes, an exquisitely chiseled face with prominent high cheekbones, a wide mouth, and a figure that was at once generous and yet athletic. Her real name was Evita Klein. She was an Argentine citizen of German extraction and spoke Spanish and German as well as faintly accented English.

Inside her dressing-room trailer, she poured coffee from an insulated carafe and handed a cup to Columbo without asking if he wanted it.

"If you want to know if I murdered Len, I was at dinner with friends all evening, at Fonda la Paloma. If you want to know if my ex-husband did it, he was in New York last Thursday evening. Or so I understand; you can check it."

"Well, your former husband did express himself pretty firmly about Mr. Wylie."

"Yes, he said he'd like to kill him. But I much doubt that he did. He has always been a talker, not a doer. Bluff is his stock in trade, Lieutenant Columbo."

"Mr. Wylie—"

"Was a doer, not a talker. I don't need to explain what I mean, do I?"

She grabbed a pack of Marlboros from a table, snapped a lighter, and drew flame into the cigarette. With that, Columbo pulled a cigar from his raincoat pocket. "Uh . . . Can I have a light?"

She handed him her lighter. "I think you can probably understand what I'm going to tell you, Lieutenant. I've never held and do not hold the slightest resentment against Len: against Tim. He was a kind and tender lover. And I wouldn't be what I am if not for him. He promised me he would help me in my career, and he did."

"So you don't hold anything against him at all? But I guess your husband did."

"My husband was a jealous fool. He was possessive. He's a photographer, you know, and got it in his mind that because he got me spreads in *Playboy* and the like, he owned me. I'd had some small film and TV exposure, but Len arranged real opportunities for me. It was the kind of thing that makes a big difference. There are thousands of us who wait and hope for a break. Len got me mine. I cried some genuine tears when I found out he'd been murdered. Now they say the art is fake— God, Lieutenant, why would anyone want to hurt him?"

"I thank ya for the coffee, Ma'am. It's very good. I won't take any more of your time."

"My time is your time."

"Well, thank ya again. This investigation has got me chances to interview some famous people."

He opened the trailer door and squinted at the Pacific and the waves coming in and breaking. "Did Mr. Wylie ever mention Miss Björling?"

"He mentioned Tammy. He told me she was his daughter, though he never met her. He told me that in absolute confidence, and I would never have betrayed that confidence, except that it's now been betrayed in the news. He wept over her, Lieutenant. Can you believe that? I bet that's a different impression of the man than you're getting from some sources."

"Right . . . Yeah, I guess that's right. Well—" He stepped down from the trailer. "Oh. Oh, say, Miss Cline. One other thing. I, uh . . . Y' understand, of course, that your former husband threatening Mr. Wylie could be an important point the defense might want to make when Miss Björling comes to trial. Has Mr. Kellogg called you?"

She shook her head. "No. No, he hasn't."

Columbo nodded. "Well . . . prob'ly doesn't mean anything. But I'd appreciate it if you'd let me know if he does."

11:49 A.M.

The store on South Olive Street looked like a place where they wouldn't object to a cigar, so Columbo walked in, enjoying the last few puffs from the stub. The place was, in fact, a sporting-goods store, where they sold everything from running shoes to handguns.

For some reason, the boy behind the counter impressed him as a smart aleck. Maybe he wasn't, but that was how he looked to Columbo. "Is Mr. Moore in?" he asked the boy.

The kid *was* a smart aleck. "Who wants to see him?"

"Lieutenant Columbo, Homicide Squad, LAPD."

The boy shrugged. "He might see you."

Columbo's eyes narrowed. "He'll see me, sonny. And right now. Where is he?"

"Hey, Arnie! Wanta talk to th' fuzz?"

Arnold Moore was not the wise guy his clerk was. He was a small, pudgy man with a belly that shoved his open-collared white shirt out over his belt buckle. His face was chubby, and his dark hair curled thinly over a pate that was soon going to be exposed entirely. He had the air of a man who felt himself harassed. He came from the back of the store and faced Columbo with a skeptical stare.

"I'm Lieutenant Columbo, LAPD, Homicide."

Moore nodded. "Lookin' into the death of that scuzzball bum Wylie. I saw your name in the paper."

Columbo turned to the smart kid, who stood staring and listening. He jerked his thumb. "Buzz off, boy." He turned to Moore. "Your name came up."

"I suppose so. What can I do for you, Lieutenant?"

"The story is, you threatened to kill Tim Wylie."

"I'm kinda sorry I didn't."

"You got an office where we can talk alone?"

"Sure. This way."

The office was on the second floor, a small, littered room at one end of a large area used as a warehouse. Moore led Columbo inside and closed the door.

"I think I know why, but tell me why you threatened to kill Wylie," said Columbo.

Moore opened a desk drawer and pulled out a bottle of

bourbon. He offered, but Columbo shook his head, and Moore took a swig from the bottle. "You got a daughter, Lieutenant Columbo?"

Columbo nodded.

"What would you do—hey, what would you *feel* like doin'—if a man almost seventy years old got in your six-teen-year-old daughter's pants?"

"That's what the law is for, Mr. Moore."

"He'd of denied it; she'd of denied it. Which didn't make it any less true."

"Is she okay now?"

"She's not a virgin. Well . . . she's seventeen now, and I don't suppose she would be a virgin anymore in any case. She was broken up when she heard of his murder. So was I. I figured I'd hear from you sooner or later. I got a good alibi for last Thursday night. I took my wife to the movies. Another couple went with us."

"I guess I can forget about you," Columbo said.

"Don't forget about Natalie." Moore opened a desk drawer and pulled out a framed photograph. It was of an extraordinarily beautiful girl: blond, with an impish face and a womanly figure, posing proudly in a brief bikini. "You can see why he wanted her. And for her— Well, hell, man. One of the biggest stars Hollywood ever produced. She thought she'd died and gone to heaven. Lieutenant . . . he got her pregnant." Moore blinked hard, and tears came from his eyes. "He got her an abortion. And he gave her twenty-five thousand dollars, cash, plus twenty for me. I shouldn't have taken it, but I did. I'm glad he's dead. I'm only sorry it was so quick and easy for him."

"Would it be possible for me to talk to Natalie?"

"Wouldn't hurt her anymore. Couldn't hurt her any-more. What do you want to know?"

"Anything he might have told her."

Moore began to write on a little notepad. "This is our address," he said. "Stop by when I'm home, too, okay? Like—?"

"How 'bout this evening?"

SIXTEEN

1

Wednesday, April 19—3:10 P.M.

Grant Kellogg came out to the reception area to greet Lieutenant Columbo.

"Lieutenant! Nice to see you. How long's it been? Not since the O'Banion case, huh?"

"You got me on that one, Mr. Kellogg. I was really sure he was guilty."

"Hey! Columbo! Between you and me—and I'll deny it if you quote me—he *was* guilty. But . . . I know you understand. It's my job, my professional and ethical obligation, to mount the best defense I can. I'm sorry I had to cross-examine you pretty hard. I hope there's no hard feelings about it."

"Naw, naw, not at all. It's all part of the job: mine and yours."

"Well, listen, I appreciate your coming."

"I got your phone message."

"Well come on in. God, I wish we had time to sit and

reminisce about old times. Maybe someday soon. Over dinner. Mrs. Columbo invited. And—" Grant grinned broadly. "The fourth for that dinner will be Erika Björling."

"I'm not sure she'll want to talk with me. I'm the guy who had the cuffs put on her."

"Did you feel sorry for her, Lieutenant? Off the record?"

Columbo nodded. "I feel sorry for a lot of people when I have to do that to 'em."

"Anyway, have a seat."

Columbo sat down on the leather-covered couch that faced Grant Kellogg's desk.

"I appreciate your coming. The DA cleared it, said we can talk mano a mano."

"Right. I checked with him before I came."

"Would you like to hang up your raincoat?"

"Well, no. Actually, y' see, it's sort of like my office. I got things in the pockets."

Grant smiled. "Okay. I'm entitled to disclosure of the evidence in possession of the police, you know. So I'm going to ask you a few questions. If you think I'm prying, you're right; I am; I have to. You understand. I need to know just what is the case against Erika."

"Well, Sir—" Columbo ticked off the points on his fingers. "In the first place, there's the note. Then there's the witness that says she was at the King's Court Motel. Then there's the fact that she told us she didn't leave her apartment until eight o'clock, which doesn't jibe with the fact that she had three calls on her answering machine between seven and eight. If she was there, she wasn't answering her phone, but she says she *always* answered her phone."

"And that's it? That's all you've got against her?"

"That's about it. The note we found in Mr. Wylie's bedroom is in Miss Björling's handwriting."

"What about fingerprints?"

"No fingerprints. But fingerprints don't always show up on paper."

Grant frowned. "I'm relieved. The case against her is not very strong."

"Y' understand, I'm not finished."

"The DA warned me of that. He didn't have to warn me. I know how you work, Lieutenant."

"Slow and steady. Uh . . . Is there anything else, Mr. Kellogg?"

"I just wanted to know if I'm going to get any surprises."

Columbo rose. "Oh, no. No. Uh— Say, could I ask *you* a question? There's something' I'm curious about."

Grant Kellogg grinned. "Ask away."

"Well, Sir, what I'm curious about has got nothing' to do with the case, I don't think. It's just something' that bothers me. I get things in my mind and— Anyway, it's none of my business, I guess, but I couldn't help wondering why it was that on the morning Miss Björling was in jail and awful anxious to see you, you went out for a boat ride. Like I say, it's none of my business, but—"

"Why do you think I took my boat out that morning?"

"I don't know. That's why I asked. If you'd been available Friday morning, she could have been arraigned then. As it was, she didn't get arraigned until Monday morning."

"What's the difference, Lieutenant? I knew and she knew that she was not going to be released on bail. So whether she was arraigned on Friday or Monday didn't make a bit of difference."

"Yeah. Well— It was a pretty blustery day, as I recall."

"And I went out on my boat, Lieutenant, because it *was* blustery, with seas running. It's how I *relax*. I knew I had a damned rough week coming, starting a defense for Erika, and I took the time to get away and go out to sea and think."

Columbo nodded. "Well, I'm glad you explained it to me. I figured there had to be some logical explanation. I thank ya."

2

6:15 P.M.

The yellow stucco house was small and square, with a pair of stately palms in front. If a house could be typical of Los Angeles, this was it. Southern California architecture, duplicated ten thousand times. It sat on a quarter-acre lot and still had room behind for a little swimming pool set in a miniature tropical garden guarded by a stone wall.

Natalie Moore conspicuously reveled in her eroticism. She chose to meet a Los Angeles homicide detective at poolside in the kind of bathing suit that had once been called a thong—this one violet. No wonder her father had insisted on being present when Columbo interviewed her. Columbo was glad he had.

"Tim was a wonderful man," she said. She flipped the ends of her blond hair with the fingers of her right hand. "We've lost a real American hero."

Arnold Moore shook his head.

"Do you know anything about why he was killed?"

"That bitch Erika Björling was insanely jealous of every other girl he saw. He told me. She was always calling him, raising hell with him. She wanted money, too."

"He told you that?" Columbo asked skeptically.

"She claimed he was the father of her kid, and she figured that some way it gave her the right to money from him."

"Her daughter has been dead six years, Natalie," said Arnold Moore.

"Makes no difference. Erika was *blackmailing* Tim!"

"Pillow talk," said Arnold Moore.

"Guys say things . . . " The girl grinned. "Y' want the truth out of a guy?" She laughed.

"Slut."

The girl glanced at her father; then her eyes returned to Columbo. "My father thinks Tim was a seducer, nothing but a seducer. But let me tell you something, Lieutenant." She glared at her father. "If he hadn't interfered—my daddy, the protective father—Tim would have made me a *star!* I could have been—"

"You'd of been the mother of his child," said Arnold.

"I'd of been *proud* to be the mother of his baby! He was the greatest American since . . . well, since maybe General MacArthur."

"Yeah, well it was Wylie that wanted the abortion," her father grunted.

"He said I was too young. He cared about me. He was going to make me *somebody.*"

Arnold Moore stared at Columbo and shook his head. He pulled a Budweiser from an ice chest and popped it open. He offered it to Columbo, but Columbo waved it away, and Moore tipped it to his own mouth. "What've I got for a daughter?" he pleaded.

"I wanta ask one more question," said Columbo. "Has either one of you had a call from Mr. Grant Kellogg?"

Both shook their heads.

"Well, let me know if you do, will ya? I'd appreciate it."

SEVENTEEN

1

Thursday, April 20—9:10 A.M.

Her clothes had been brought to the jail, so Erika wore her black suit and white blouse on the van ride to the courthouse. Also, someone had apparently decided it was not necessary to chain her legs, so she was wearing only handcuffs and a belly chain when she arrived for her first appearance before the Superior Court.

"How's it going?" Grant asked her when she had been unchained and sat down beside him in the courtroom. "Haven't talked to you since Tuesday."

She fixed a stare on him. "I am now a jailhouse laundry sorter," she said grimly. "I also have cellmates: one prostitute, one marijuana farmer, and a professional automobile thief."

"To whom you don't talk," said Grant emphatically.

"I've got a *little* smarts."

"I've got a million-dollar offer," he told her. "I'm gonna raise it before the court this morning. I think it's going to need a court order."

"A million dollars . . . "

"You still insist I give notice of alibi this morning?"

She nodded. "Grant, I'm *scared*. What if Sonya and Freddy backed out?"

"They won't back out. I haven't paid them yet."

"They may get cold feet. You got to put their names out. Once they're publicly identified, they—"

"It's a bad tactic. It's too soon."

"Grant . . . "

He sighed and shrugged. "Okay, kiddo."

"They might even drop the case, once they know we've got five alibi witnesses."

"God forbid! Not until we get our million dollars."

Judge Frank Reynolds entered the courtroom. He was a pudgy, red-faced man in his sixties.

The judge looked at his notes. "Let the record show that the defendant, Miss Erika Björling, is present before the court, with her counsel, Mr. Grant Kellogg. The People of California are represented by Mr. Charles Dunedin. Mr. Kellogg—?"

Grant rose. "I have two matters to present, Your Honor. The second is routine. The first is somewhat unusual."

"Proceed with the unusual, Mr. Kellogg," said the judge dryly.

Grant nodded. "Your Honor, my client Miss Björling is in a difficult situation. She is not in such economic circumstances that she can ask for defense by the Public Defender. On the other hand, her circumstances are such that it will be difficult—no, Your Honor, it will be impossible—for her to mount a thorough and effective defense from her present financial resources. I refer in part to my fees, of course; but I refer also to the many and heavy costs of defending against a charge of murder. I am prepared, Your Honor, to postpone indefinitely the collection of my fees, or even to waive them, but the cost of transcripts, research, co-counsel, expert witnesses, and so on will quickly exhaust the defendant's resources. It is not an unusual situation, Your Honor—a person who is not poor but is far from rich can find himself, herself, at an overwhelming disadvantage.

"In Miss Björling's situation, however, there may be salvation. She is a celebrity. The man she is alleged to have murdered was a star. The media— Well, Your Honor, I need hardly tell you. You and I ran a gauntlet to get into the courthouse this morning. A number of media organizations have offered substantial money for an exclusive interview with Miss Björling in jail. Sybil Brand Institute has not refused to allow such an interview, but I fear it will— not from arbitrary motives but out of fear that a precedent will be set. I respectfully move the court to issue an order allowing such an interview, or interviews."

"On what legal ground do you base your motion, Mr. Kellogg?"

"On the basis that denying Miss Björling the right to be interviewed in the jail denies her the only source she presently has to raise funds essential for her defense."

"Mr. Dunedin, will the People object?"

"We do not object, Your Honor—provided the order specifically limits the interviews to nondisruptive times and settings."

"Counsel will draft an order acceptable to both sides. If it is acceptable to me, I will sign it. And your second item of business, Mr. Kellogg?"

"If the court please, I would like at this time to present a notice of alibi and a list of alibi witnesses. I realize of course that this need not be done in open court, and I will serve the notice and list on the District Attorney in the ordinary way. For now, however, Your Honor, I offer notice that the defendant will plead an alibi and will call five witnesses to testify that she was at a bowling alley more than thirty miles from Bel Air at nine o'clock that evening."

"What is the significance of that, Mr. Kellogg?"

"Your Honor, the coroner has fixed the time of death of Tim Wylie as approximately eight-thirty. Miss Björling could not have driven from the Wylie home in Bel Air to the Ten Strikes Bowling Alley in Long Beach in less than forty-five minutes, and it would more likely have taken an hour. The prosecution is also suggesting that Miss Björling checked out of a Bel Air motel at approximately eight-forty-five. If that is true, it gives the defendant fifteen minutes to reach the bowling alley thirty miles away."

Charles Dunedin stood. "Your Honor, that defense will depend on the veracity of the alibi witnesses."

"Precisely," said the judge. "An issue to be determined by the jury. Is there anything else?"

Charles Dunedin stood. "Your Honor, the People would like an order to United California Bank, Van Nuys, allowing us to examine the defendant's checking-account records."

"Mr. Kellogg?"

"No objection, Your Honor."

When the court adjourned, Grant spoke quietly to Erika. "I've arranged for a photographer to be in the hall where they take you out to the van. I want him to get a shot of you with the cuffs on. Harry Gottsman will pay us $20,000 for it. Front page of *PROBE*."

Erika sighed and shook her head, but she said, "Alright."

"Listen, one more thing. Harry Gottsman will pay some really important money for nude or topless photos of you. Are there any?"

Erika shook her head.

"I figured that. Look, I can get a photo lab to fake them—I mean, put your head on another body. If you don't deny them, we can sell them as real."

"Is there any end to how much I have to be humiliated?"

He shrugged. "Is it a deal?"

She closed her eyes and sighed. "Okay. If I'm doing everything else I'm doing for the money, I might as well do that."

10:16 A.M.

Columbo and Captain Sczciegel sat across a desk from Assistant District Attorney Charles Dunedin. Although the young lawyer was barely thirty years old, he wore bifocals: *rimless* bifocals. He carried a package of cigarettes in his vest pocket, and he lit a cigarette.

"Can I borrow your lighter for a minute?" asked Columbo.

Dunedin handed him the lighter, and Columbo lit a fresh new cigar.

"Linda Delgardo, Michael Finn, Fred Mansfield, Sonya Pavlov, and Hugo Wilson. Who do you suppose *they* are, Lieutenant Columbo?"

"Well, Sir, I'd guess those are people who'll say they saw Miss Björling at the Ten Strikes Bowling Alley last Thursday night."

Dunedin stared at Columbo with the air of a man looking at a mental defective. "Of course they are. But *who are they?*"

"That's what I'm gonna have to find out."

"If these are reliable people, who really did see her, we lose the case, you understand."

"Which would take us back to square one as to who killed Tim Wylie," Sczciegel said unhappily.

"I sure wouldn't like to be wrong about this," said Columbo.

"You need help?"

"Well, Jesús Ruiz will be workin' with me. He's a good man. We'll interview these witnesses. It's one thing to file notices; it's another thing to back 'em up with good witnesses."

"She *did* say she was at this bowling alley, from the very beginning, didn't she?" Dunedin asked.

"Right. We'll check it out. Lemme change the subject. On Monday Miss Brinsley's column named two men she said had a motive to kill Tim Wylie. Now, there's a strong defense for Mr. Kellogg to use. Well, here it is Thursday, and he hasn't contacted Miss Cline or her ex-husband, or Miss Moore or her father. I checked with 'em by phone ten minutes ago. Don'tcha think that's a little odd?"

"What do you expect to find in Erika Björling's bank account, Lieutenant?"

"Miss Moore says Mr. Wylie told her Miss Björling was blackmailing him. I'm lookin' for big unexplained deposits."

3

12:38 P.M.

"Jesús, you'll never learn to play pool if you insist on shootin' so *hard*."

"The truth is, Lieutenant, I'll never learn to shoot pool."

"Or to like Burt's chili," Columbo said with a grin. "Well, the French got a word for it. Somethin' like . . . Well, I can't remember it right now."

"*Chacun à son goût,*" said Jesús.

"That's it. You must've gone to college. Anyway—"

"Michael Reilly. He's in the phone book. I called and got his wife, and she told me where he works: produce manager in a supermarket. So I went there and talked to him. He definitely saw Erika Björling that evening. In fact, the lounge manager introduced him to her. But he's not sure what time. He bowled with his bowling league and afterward went into the lounge for a beer. The woman who manages the cocktail lounge is Sonya Pavlov. He's taking her word as to what time it was. I got the names of some of the other members of his bowling league. I figure on asking them what time they finished their game."

"Good thinkin', Jesús."

"Then there's Hugo Wilson. I hit it lucky this morning and got to talk to two of these witnesses before noon. Dr. Wilson is a chiropractor. He's very anxious to cooperate. He confirms that he absolutely did see Erika Björling in the lounge at Ten Strikes on the evening of the murder."

"What time? That's the important thing. What time did he see her?"

Ruiz smiled. "He's not sure. I asked him what he could testify to, as to the time. He said sometime between nine and ten, and he couldn't be sure if it was closer to nine or ten. Scratch one alibi witness."

"Had these fellows ever seen her there before?"

"Uh . . . no. But they couldn't testify she had never before been there when they were at the bar. The place is dimly lighted. Reilly said he could have overlooked a friend sitting in one of the booths."

"Then how did he notice Erika Björling?" Columbo asked.

"The bartender pointed her out to him."

"What about Dr. Wilson?"

"Sonya Pavlov told him to look who was sitting over there."

"Well, it makes a whole lot of difference," said Columbo. "If Erika Björling was there at nine, she couldn't have killed Tim Wylie at eight-thirty and driven all the way to Long Beach. If she was there at nine-thirty, she could have."

"These two witnesses aren't going to do the defense much good," said Sergeant Ruiz.

"Go for Linda Delgardo. I guess I'll have to pop by Ten Strikes tonight."

"Okay. Oh— Tuesday I called on Melvin Glassman— Tim Wylie's ex-son-in-law. Thanks for the assignment. I thought he was going to throttle me, detective or no detective. Anyway, yesterday I was able to confirm his story. He didn't leave his office until almost eight, then went to dinner with his girlfriend and was in the restaurant until nine-thirty or a quarter till ten. They were seen together by the headwaiter, their waiter, and the bartender."

"Good. Glad to get that one out of the way."

EIGHTEEN

1

Thursday, April 20—2:13 P.M.

Erika pulled out an orange fiberglass chair and sat down, facing Grant through a heavy screen. Seeing him through the screen and not in one of the private lawyer-client rooms freed her from two strip searches.

"What's the urgency?" he asked.

"I got to thinking. They're going to find something bad when they go over my bank records."

"What?"

"Deposits. *Cash* deposits. What little income I've had since the show was canceled has all been in the form of checks. But I made two cash deposits. One for two thousand. One for five."

"What were they?"

"Money from Len."

"*My God!* You didn't tell me you got money from Len!"

Erika blinked, and tears gleamed in the corners of her eyes. "Well, I did."

"Who could know it?"

"Nobody but him. Unless he told somebody."

"How'd you get it out of him?"

"By telling him I'd go to a tabloid with the story of who was Tammy's father."

"You *blackmailed* him!"

"If you want to call it that."

"Well, what else would you call it?" Grant asked angrily. He drew a deep breath. "We're going to have to make up some kind of story to explain where you got that much cash. Or . . . or maybe it would be a good idea just to admit you got the money from him. We can say he felt sorry for you. We can say it was a loan. Your defense relies on the alibi witnesses."

"Grant . . . I'm *scared.*"

"I'll have to think about this. Maybe they won't ask. But— Tell me, Erika. Do I have any more surprises coming? The worst thing that can happen to a defense lawyer is to get surprised. Is there anything more I need to know?"

She shook her head.

2

5:16 P.M.

Peg Brinsley greeted Columbo effusively. "To what do I owe the pleasure of two visits in one week by a handsome homicide detective? Come in! Come in and let me pour you a drink. It is cocktail hour, after all."

"Well, just a very light Scotch. I'm on duty, and I'm beginnin' to think I—"

"Lieutenant Columbo, let me tell you something. I never trust a man who doesn't drink, on duty or off."

"Cigars are more my vice."

"Well, vodka is mine."

She went to her bar. Again, in the privacy of her apartment, she did not wear a wig, and her bald head served as a monument to her individuality. She was wearing something he guessed was out of style: black velvet toreador pants with a white polo shirt. Again, she was an *individual*.

Columbo put his raincoat aside and sat down. "I asked to talk with you again because I figure you know more about the inside stories than anybody else I could ask."

"You figure I got the skinny," she said.

"I figure you do, Ma'am."

"So what do you want to know?"

"Coupla things, if you don't mind. In the first place, when I talked to Natalie Moore, she claimed Tim Wylie told her Erika Björling was blackmailing him."

"I'd be careful of that one, Columbo. Natalie's a little slut. How good's her word?"

"I get ya. This morning Mr. Kellogg filed a list of alibi witnesses. One of them is named Sonya Pavlov. She's the manager of a cocktail lounge in Long Beach. Somebody at headquarters thinks he remembers her as a television actress. Ever hear of her?"

Peg Brinsley came to the couch and sat down, placing their drinks on the coffee table. "I've heard of her. Did a few parts on television. Couldn't get more. Life's tough for a woman who makes it small in show biz. Sonya Pavlov's a hustler. Notice I said *hustler*, not hooker. She does what she has to do to make money. Which includes sleeping around. But she doesn't rent by the hour."

"I gotta go interview her. This'll be helpful."

"She's a good-looking woman and has a cute accent. Russian, I think. Managing a cocktail lounge . . . I'd think she could do better."

"This'll be very helpful."

"Uh . . . Alibi witness. Hell, yes! Hey, Columbo! I said she slept around. Now that I think of it, there was a rumor one time that she had an affair with Grant Kellogg."

"Y' don't say. Uh . . . Ma'am, I don't mean to impose, but could I make one local call on your telephone?"

She grinned. "Columbo, you can call Timbuktu on my telephone, if you want to."

"Won't take a minute."

She handed him a cordless phone, and he made the call from there on her couch. He called in to see if he had any messages. He had one. A detective sergeant read it to him—

"It's from Sergeant Ruiz, Lieutenant. It says, 'Spoke with Linda Delgardo. Same story. Uncertain of time. But adds that Grant Kellogg arrived before she left about 11:30 and that he spoke with EB as well as with SP.' "

7:20 P.M.

"I thought you'd be around," said Sonya Pavlov. "Mr. Kellogg warned me."

The woman Columbo faced was what Peg Brinsley had told him to look for: an attractive middle-aged blond with a light accent. She wore black tights and a white knit shirt.

He sat at the bar.

"He didn't have to warn you against me, Ma'am. I'm not a bad fellow."

"He said you are the toughest detective with LAPD."

Columbo grinned and ran his hand through his hair. "Nah. Naw. Not me. I'm just an ordinary workin' cop. That's been my life."

"I bet you've got questions for me."

"Well, maybe. One or two."

"How 'bout a drink on the house?"

"I shouldn't do that, Ma'am. I—"

"Beer? Something else?"

"Well, maybe just a light Scotch. Really light, please. I gotta drive home, y' know."

"Eat some peanuts. They coat your stomach."

"Y' know, they do. I've noticed that. Anyway, do you mind telling me how long you've known Miss Björling?"

"I don't know exactly. We could find out. I appeared as a contestant on *Try It Once*, and we became acquainted. She knew I wanted to make it in television or the movies. She wanted to make it bigger than she had. We had something in common."

"I can understand that. Everybody has ambitions. Most of us get 'em frustrated. Which is too bad."

She smiled lazily at him. "What would you want to be, Lieutenant Columbo, if you weren't Los Angeles's most successful homicide detective?"

"Since I'm not that, that's what I'd like to be: the most successful— Also, I'd like to get insights, like Sherlock Holmes, so I could get home to dinner on time, instead of havin' to work, work, work to get results. 'Course, tonight Mrs. Columbo's bowling, so— Well. I ramble on. Would you say Miss Björling's a friend of yours?"

"If you're asking me if I'd lie for her, the answer is no; we're not *that* good friends. But we're more than just acquaintances." Here was a word where her accent came out. She and Erika were "ack-*vaint*-un-cess."

"What I need to know is what time she got here."

"I have no question about that. She was here at nine o'clock. It could have been five before or five after, but she was here at nine o'clock."

"You don't have any doubt about the time?"

Sonya turned down the corners of her mouth and shook her head. "I have to keep track of the time. I have employees. I have to close at a certain hour. I have to know when some bowling leagues are apt to finish, so I'll have people on hand to serve a sudden new bunch of customers all coming in at once."

"Speaking of employees, does Fred Mansfield work for you?"

"Right. Sometimes I have to remind him, he works for me."

"Well, I gotta talk to him too. Is he around?"

"Not yet. He's having trouble with his girlfriend and asked for some time off this evening. He'll be in later."

"I guess you're gonna be the chief alibi witness."

She shrugged. "Maybe you could say that."

Columbo raised his eyebrows and nodded. "Did you call Mr. Kellogg or did he call you?"

"I didn't have to call him. He was here that night. He talked to Erika and to me. When she was charged, both of us realized that I was a witness who had seen her here when she was supposed to be in Bel Air."

"Okay. Oh . . . Say. there is one more thing I ought to ask you. Little thing. Prob'ly doesn't amount to anything. I wonder, though. Isn't it good for business to have people like Erika Björling and Grant Kellogg comin' in for drinks? I mean, people like that you don't usually see in bowling-alley bars. Right?"

"We get celebrities from time to time," she said.

"Sure. You got a nice bar here, Ma'am. But I wonder. When you get a celebrity in here, I wonder if you make a point of sayin' to your regular customers somethin' like, 'Hey, look who's over there. Looka there. That's Erika Björling. That's Grant Kellogg.' Do you do that?"

She shrugged. "I suppose so."

"So you kinda made a point, maybe, of pointin' out to people that was here—like you didn't want anybody to miss her."

"Erika's a celebrity. Having her in here *is* good for business, and I *do* point her out."

Columbo nodded. "I wondered. I can understand. That explains why you did that. I knew there'd be some logical reason why you did. 'Course, that was lucky for Mr. Kellogg. It gave him five alibi witnesses, 'steada one or two."

"If you say so."

"If he'd got there a little earlier, he could've been an alibi witness himself, couldn't he? Popular place, this bar. Seems like everybody was here that night—defendant, defense counsel, and all the alibi witnesses. Must've been kind of convenient for Mr. Kellogg."

Sonya Pavlov frowned stiffly. "At that point, Lieutenant Columbo, no one could have guessed that Erika would be charged with the murder of Tim Wylie."

Columbo raised a hand. "You gotta good point there, Miss Pavlov. I 'preciate your reminding me of that."

NINETEEN

1

"Uh, Sir, I'm Lieutenant Columbo, Los Angeles Police Department, Homicide. I b'lieve you got an order—"

The banker nodded, and there was no misunderstanding the hostility on his face. "We did, Lieutenant. The information is on computer tapes. Will you want it printed out?"

"You're Mister—?"

"McDonald. Philip McDonald. Will you come this way?"

Columbo followed McDonald, who might have worn morning trousers and a cutaway, so formal was he, but was actually wearing a black three-piece suit. He might also have been wearing a pince-nez and a pencil mustache but was actually without eyeglasses and had a bland, pudgy face. He led into the bowels of the bank, so to speak, into the coldly lighted working rooms where people and computers labored.

He drew up two chairs to two sides of an attractive young woman who sat at a computer terminal. He handed her an account number, she typed it in, and shortly a portion of the Björling account glowed on the screen.

"Where would you like to start, Lieutenant Columbo?"

"Can we start with now and go back?" Columbo asked, pointing right to left.

The young woman tapped some keys, and the most current information on the account appeared.

"What I'm lookin' for is deposits," said Columbo. "Does it show if deposits were made in cash?"

She tapped keys, and the deposits appeared on the screen.

"What's that there?" Columbo asked, pointing at a five-thousand-dollar deposit made in January. "Was that cash?"

The young woman nodded. "Cash. Five thousand in cash."

"Right. Are there any more like that?"

"Well, here's another one. Two thousand in cash, November of last year. And— And there don't seem to be any more."

"Well— That's *excellent*. That's just what I was lookin' for. You don't need to print that right now. The District Attorney's office will be in touch about the form they'll need that in, to make it evidence admissible in court."

"We are always happy to extend cooperation to the police," said McDonald.

2

11:20 A.M.

Victoria Glassman sat at her father's desk, in his study in the house of North Perugia Way.

"Y' understand, we can get this information from the

bank," Columbo said. "It did seem, though, like a simpler way would be to look into his bank statements. I appreciate your consenting."

Vicky Glassman had shown up in white shorts and an emerald-green golf shirt. Her mother had chosen to sit by the pool sipping a Bloody Mary and let her daughter and the detective pry into anything they wanted to pry into.

"I'm looking for two withdrawals. One in January was for five thousand dollars. One in November was for two thousand."

Vicky looked directly into his eyes. "Since I'm cooperating with you, I think you might tell me what you're trying to find out."

"Well— I want to see if he withdrew those amounts at about the same time Miss Björling made deposits of the same amounts, in cash."

"And why—?"

"Somebody has suggested she was blackmailing him."

Vicky flushed. "Yeah. Why shouldn't she? Others did."

"Well, Ma'am—"

"Let's look at something besides checking-account statements." She flipped through a folder. "Here. Smith Barney, financial management account. Let's see . . . January 9. Withdrawal of five thousand. November last year . . . There you are!"

"Could be coincidence."

"Sure it could," she said bitterly. "You believe that, you believe in the tooth fairy."

Columbo wrinkled his nose. "Nah, thanks," he said.

Adrienne laughed. "Didn't think so. But you ought to try it sometime. Bumper pool takes some skill."

"It's okay for *them.*" He nodded at the topless waitresses who worked in the Oscar and would play bumper pool with any customer who asked them. "Not real pool."

"Okay," Adrienne conceded. "But my innards just couldn't take another bowl of Burt's chili. I wondered if we couldn't try a game of bumper pool, after which we could have a decent lunch. Listen. You say you like anything that comes from the sea. Well . . . You like abalone?"

"I like anything that comes from the sea. Abalone? A special favorite."

"We'll have it. C'mon now. Check the raincoat. There are no dread secrets of LAPD in the pockets, are there?"

"Well . . . If the check girl isn't careful she'll break the shell on my hard-boiled egg."

"Columbo!"

"They make nice snacks during the day."

They sat down at a table. It overlooked a swimming pool and paddleball courts.

"Kellogg is peddling the rights to an exclusive jailhouse interview with Erika Björling. He's promising she'll be inside a cell, and the camera will look at her through bars. He's put it up for auction. The minimum bid has to be one million dollars. Columbo! This is what you call *exploitation.*"

"What's she gonna do, tell something more? What's she gonna say, that she also got pregnant by—?"

"No, she's going to tell what a horrible experience it is to be in jail. It's for *voyeurs,* Columbo! What the hell are they trying to do? They're peddling the story for all it's worth—and a hell of a lot more—and she hasn't even been *tried,* much less acquitted."

"How's the old saying go? 'Something is rotten in the state of Denmark.' Is that Shakespeare, Adrienne? Yeah. Shakespeare. I'm a great admirer of Shakespeare, go to any movie that's a Shakespeare play."

Adrienne laughed and shook her head. "Columbo, I will never figure you out. Neither will anybody else."

3:17 P.M.

On his hands and knees behind the '91 Toyota, Columbo stretched as far as he could and still could not reach the smear of fluid that lay on the pavement of the apartment-house garage. He stood up and walked outside. Ah! The edges of the driveway were littered with twigs. What he needed. He picked up a twig and returned to the garage. Thrusting it forward he reached the fluid and pulled the stick back with a sample clinging to it.

"Do you mind if I ask what the hell you're doing?"

Columbo rose and faced a burly man in a white T-shirt: burly and fat, with belly hanging out over his belt. He was not friendly. He wanted to know what the guy in the rain-coat was doing on the garage floor.

"I was lookin' at this here liquid that's dripping out of this car. Y' know? That doesn't look like oil. Doesn't smell like oil. What is that, y' s'pose?"

"It's transmission fluid. Miss Pavlov's car leaks transmission fluid. So what business is that of yours?"

Columbo grinned and shook his head. "No business of mine at all, Sir. It's just that— Well, y' see, my car drips the same way, this stuff that's not oil. That's my car, out there on the street. It's a French car, like you see; and when I noticed this foreign car drippin' the same way mine does— Well, I wanted to see why."

"What are you doing in this garage anyway?"

"Well, Sir, y' see . . . You're not Mr. Blake, by any chance?"

"No, I'm not."

"You know Mr. Blake?"

The man shook his head.

"Well, y' see, what I am is, I'm a repossessor. I mean, I'm in the business of taking back cars people don't pay for. Not a very well-liked job, but somebody's got to do it. Y' know? Anyway, I was in here lookin' for this car I've got to repossess, and— Well, I saw this car drippin' the same way mine does, so—"

"Okay, it's drippin' transmission fluid. It's been doing it for a year."

"Can't you get that fixed?" Columbo asked.

"Have the gasket replaced."

"Is that expensive?"

"Apparently more than Miss Pavlov can afford."

"Oh. Well, that's too bad. Listen, I thank ya. Transmission fluid. I better have my gasket fixed right away. Losin' fluid like that could damage your car, right?"

"Right."

"Well, I thank ya again. I better be goin'. Uh . . . Maybe I could give Miss— What'd you say her name is? Pavlov? Maybe I could call her this evening and ask her what it would cost her to get her gasket replaced. It'd cost me about the same, wouldn't it?"

"Go in and ask her now. She's home, obviously. She works nights and sometimes doesn't come home at all." The fat man grinned. "I think she's got a friend."

"Well . . . If she works nights, she's prob'ly getting her rest right now. I guess I'll just ask my mechanic."

5

4:11 P.M.

Columbo walked up the driveway of the little house where Grant Kellogg lived in Pasadena. He squatted and ran his finger across a wet smear on the driveway. He squinted at what was on his finger, and sniffed at it.

Transmission fluid.

6

5:15 P.M.

"Hiya, Donahue! How's everything? How's the missus?"

Captain John Donahue grabbed Columbo's hand and shook it with warmth and enthusiasm. He was a small, sandy-haired man with bulging pale-blue eyes. He was in uniform.

"Columbo, you old son of a gun! How's the guy with the best job on the Force?"

"Why do I got the best job?"

"You get to hobnob with all the celebrities, some of 'em the best-lookin' women in town."

"All in the line of duty, Donahue; all in the line of duty."

"Well, sit down. I bet there's something I can do for you. You wouldn't come to see me if there wasn't."

"Yeah. Well I wrote a note down here— Where's my notebook? It's in one of these pockets. I made a point of— Ah, here. Lemme tear this out and give it to you. That's an address, and that's a license number. You're the watch commander. I'd appreciate it if you'd have a black-and-white go past that house a few times tonight, lookin' for that car. When the next watch comes on, I'd appreciate it if they'd do it, too. That car's more likely to show up after midnight. And if it does, then I'd like to know when it leaves. Not exactly, y' understand, just whether it leaves before or after dawn."

Donahue frowned over the note. "I know this address. Let's see—"

"Mr. Grant Kellogg."

"And the car belongs to—?"

"His chief alibi witness in the Erika Björling case."

Donahue laughed. "Columbo, you're a dog!"

"Be an interestin' development, wouldn't it?"

"The man couldn't be that dumb."

Columbo lifted his chin and grinned. "Prob'ly not. But maybe. Ego can make a man careless."

"We'll keep an eye on it."

7

8:32 P.M.

Her dormitory was in lock, and Erika and her cellmates were confined to their cell.

The auto thief lay on her cot with her hands clasped behind her head and stared at the ceiling. She spent a lot of time doing just that. She was a black woman with a café-au-lait complexion. Her name was Miriam.

The prostitute worked on her fingernails. She was not in jail for prostitution but for cutting one of her johns with a switchblade knife and relieving him of his money. She said she'd done it because he refused to pay what he'd agreed to pay for her services. She figured she was justified, and she was confident a jury would think so, too. She was a hard-edged blond. Her name was Pearl.

The young woman charged with farming half an acre of marijuana and selling it by the kilo lounged against the bars with her hands clasped outside. She pressed her face to the bars sometimes and tried to see up and down the corridor. She was a softly plump little girl with long dark hair. As was the case with Erika, this was her first jail experience. Her name was Lily.

Erika leaned against the cell door, gripping one of the cold steel bars with her right hand. She had been in here a week. It seemed as if she'd never been anywhere else.

"Are they going to bring a television camera in here?" Lily asked.

"Not in here," said Erika. "If we're allowed to do it, it will be some other place, some other cell. I'll be alone."

"I don't want to be on television."

"You won't be."

"I wouldn't mind," Pearl said. "Might be good for business."

"Where you're goin', you won't be doin' any business," Miriam said. "Not for a good many years. You an' me are goin' to Fontera, dear. So's Lily. Erika's the only one with a chance to walk. 'Course . . . she'll go for *life* if her jury doesn't buy her alibi witnesses."

"You scared, Erika?" Lily asked gently.

"I'm terrified."

"If I had *your* lawyer, I'd get off for sure," said Pearl.

"I hope those alibi witnesses of yours are clean," said Miriam. "If there's anything wrong with 'em—" She shook her head.

"Thanks for reminding me," Erika said bitterly.

"Were you surprised the van Gogh turned out to be a fake?" Lily asked.

"Yes. I thought his art collection was real."

"How could you make that judgment?" Lily asked.

"I'd seen it. I'd been in the house before. I mean, he *was* the father of my daughter."

Miriam rolled up her eyes and pursed her lips. " 'Before.' " she murmured to herself. " 'Before.' Hmm."

TWENTY

Saturday, April 22—9:24 A.M.

Miriam sat down in the cubicle where detectives and lawyers interviewed inmates and waited for the gumshoe they'd said would come to talk to her. Gonna meet with the fuzz, but that made no difference; she'd been strip-searched before she was allowed what they called a "contact visit."

Bastards wouldn't let her have a smoke. Goddamned righteous reformers had banned smoking in the lockups. By the time she got out of here and out of Fontera, she'd be clean of the craving for nicotine, maybe. And maybe clean of the craving for other things.

This couldn't be the detective! What had they sent her? The screw let him in. C'mon! Who the hell was this? Guy with uncombed hair. Guy wearing a shabby old raincoat. His suit wasn't so great-lookin', either, and the narrow end of his necktie hung underneath the wide end.

"Hiya," he said. "I'm Lieutenant Columbo, LAPD

Homicide. I got the call, sayin' you wanted to talk to the man in charge of the Erika Björling investigation. So . . . I'm the guy you wanta talk to."

"You . . . are . . . Columbo?"

He grinned. "Couldn't prove it by me. That's what they call me. Hey. My mother and father were named Columbo. But maybe I fell off a turnip wagon and they just took me in. You never know for sure, do ya?"

Miriam nodded. "Sure. Yeah. I've heard the name for years . . . and *you* show up. Okay. You're Columbo. You got the Erika Björling case. She's a cellmate of mine. I wanta tell you something she said last night. But of course I want you to do something for me. You know what I mean. Put the word in. I helped you."

"Can't make any promises," said Columbo. "You've had some experience. You know I can't make promises."

"No. You guys never do."

2

10:44 A.M.

Sergeant Jesús Ruiz found Columbo standing on a pier, peeling and eating a hard-boiled egg and staring at the rolling green waves.

"The dispatcher said you might be out here," said Ruiz. "Some pier, anyway. Martha suggested this one."

Columbo nodded. "Yeah. Might be here. I left word I might. Hey . . . Y' ever come out someplace like this and just stand and look at the water? Makes thinkin' easier. Y' know that? Makes thinkin' easier."

"I guess . . ."

Columbo shook his head. "Y' go out and watch the big

waves coming in on Malibu. That's not good for thinkin'. I mean watching guys get wiped out. No. But here, where it's peaceful— There's something about salt water, Jesús. Y' know, that's where they say we all come from, from the salt water."

"Yeah, Lieutenant, but I got—"

"*Ideas.* Y' gotta sort out your ideas."

"I picked up a note from Captain Donahue. It was for you, but—"

"Donahue. What's he say?"

"Lemme read it to you—"

The car that leaks transmission fluid arrived at the Pasadena address between 1:15 and 2:00. It left between 5:45 and 6:15. Helpful?

Columbo grinned. "I tell ya, Jesús. That is *helpful.* By golly, that is helpful."

11:56 A.M.

"You're not the easiest man in the world to find," Columbo said to Fred Mansfield.

"I'm at the Ten Strikes every night."

They stood outside an apartment building in Long Beach. Columbo had buzzed to be admitted, and Mansfield had said he was coming out, so hold on a minute.

"I won't take much of your time."

Fred glanced at his watch. "I hope not. I'm meeting my girl for lunch. She gets just an hour off."

"I can understand you're bein' anxious to meet her," said

Columbo. He frowned at his cigar, which had gone out, and flipped it into the street. "But you're listed in the alibi notice Mr. Kellogg filed, so I gotta talk to you."

Fred shrugged. "Talk away."

"The big question is the time. I suppose you're sure about the time. I mean, you're sure Miss Björling came in your bar pretty close to nine o'clock."

Fred nodded. "Pretty close. Give or take five or ten minutes."

"She comes in a lot?"

"Now and then."

"It's a long way from where she lives. She's gotta drive pretty close to an hour to get there. What's the attraction, y' suppose?"

"I wouldn't know—unless it's that she and Sonya are good friends."

"Old friends too, huh?"

"I guess so."

"They ever tell you where they met, and how?"

"On the beach. Sonya's a surfer, used to be big about it. She got wiped out one day, and Erika pulled her out of the water."

"Would you say that you and Erika are friends?"

"I wish I could say that. But I have to say 'acquaintances.' "

"How about you and Mr. Kellogg? How well do you know him?"

"I serve drinks to him."

"Often?"

"He comes in from time to time."

"It's a long drive for him, too. I guess you wouldn't call your bar a really big attraction, that people come from all over town to visit. Would you?"

Fred shrugged. "People come in. I don't know where they come from."

"Well, Mr. Kellogg comes from Pasadena. By the way, has he been in *since* the night of the murder?"

"Yeah, once or twice."

"I wonder what's the attraction. Since Miss Björling's in jail, he's not comin' to see *her.*"

"I guess he and Sonya are pretty good friends."

"There's a rumor that they're more than just pretty good friends."

Fred grinned. "Could be."

"A TV personality from Van Nuys and a prominent lawyer from Pasadena . . . and they get together in a bowling-alley bar in Long Beach. How 'bout Tim Wylie? He ever come in?"

"No, Lieutenant, he never did. Not that I know about. So— Is there anything else? Erika Björling came in about nine o'clock. That wasn't anything unusual. She was there. Whatta y' want me to say?"

"Nothin'. And I guess I am takin' too much of your time. You wanta go see your girl. So . . . "

"Anytime, Lieutenant." Fred gave him a dismissing little smile. "Anytime."

"I appreciate your cooperation. So, uh— Oh, say. There is one little thing I meant to ask you. None of my business, really, but— Would you mind telling me what your girl's name is?"

"It *isn't* any of your business."

"Okay. If it's a secret . . . "

"It's no secret. Her name is Mary Nelle Fiske. She's a checkout girl in a Woolworth's store, and—"

"Miss Pavlov says you and your girl are having a serious problem. That's none of my business either, but—"

"It's none of your business!"

4

"The name's Columbo. Lieutenant Columbo. LAPD homicide."

The fat man in wrinkled white shirt, red satin necktie, and gray slacks that were too small for him stared hard at Columbo's badge and ID. He was the manager of this Woolworth's store.

"Well— Can I do something' for you?"

"Yeah. I'd appreciate it if you'd let me buy a cup of coffee or a Coke for one of your employees, there at the lunch counter. In fact, now that I think of it, I haven't had any lunch. I—"

"Which employee?"

"Mary Nelle Fiske."

"Is she in some kind of trouble?"

"Oh, no, Sir. Not at all. She just might have a little bit of information that would be helpful to me. She hasn't even associated with bad people. She just might know somethin' I need to know."

The man nodded. "Take a stool, Lieutenant. I'll send her over."

Columbo sat down. "I don't know how long it's been since I've had a grilled cheese sandwich," he said to the woman behind the lunch counter. "That just does appeal. And do you have Dr. Pepper?"

"Pepsi," the woman said.

"Pepsi it is, then."

Mary Nelle Fiske came over and sat down on the next stool. She was a cute kid, as Columbo thought of her. He guessed she was eighteen, nineteen at the most. She was pretty in no particularly distinctive way. Her dishwater-blond hair was thick and curly. Her face was square. Her body was lush.

"Miss, my name is Columbo. I'm with the Los Angeles Police Department, Homicide Division."

"Freddy told me you talked to him at noon."

"Hey, I'm sorry if I made him late. You know how it is. I'm investigating a murder."

"I don't know anything about it."

"I know you don't."

"Is Freddy in some kind of trouble?"

"Oh, no, I don't think so. But he's a witness, you know, and I have to find out what I can about him. Just routine investigating, y' know."

"Freddy's a nice guy," Mary Nelle said simply and sincerely.

"I got that impression."

"A real nice guy," she said, a note of sadness coming into her voice.

Columbo ran his hand through his hair and nodded. "I get the idea some way that you and Freddy have got a problem. Some kinda personal problem that may be none of my business. Uh, coffee? Or a Pepsi? Or a sandwich, if you like. I—"

"Pepsi," she said to the woman behind the counter. She turned toward Columbo. "Yeah, a problem. The usual problem. Nothing special. It happens to everybody, I guess."

"What's that, Miss?"

Mary Nelle drew a deep breath, then showed Columbo a wan smile. "What else? I'm pregnant."

"Aw . . . well. That's not so bad, is it? Or is it?"

"It wouldn't be so bad except for one little thing. Freddy is married to somebody else."

"Uh-oh."

"Yeah. She's not a nice girl, Lieutenant Columbo. He and I could be *so happy*. But . . . She wants money. To let him go. A lot of money. And people like me and Freddy don't have that kind of money."

Columbo nodded. "I see your point. Hey, uh . . . Would you like half of a nice grilled cheese sandwich?"

TWENTY-ONE

1

Saturday, April 22—4:25 P.M.

Erika grabbed Grant's hands and clutched them tightly. "Hey, man! I can't *stand* this! You gotta get me outa here. I can't take it any more!"

Grant glanced at the guard who was watching. "Kid . . . I told you. You agreed. You've *got* to take if for a while. This is what's worth money. Hey. The million-dollar deal! It's almost in the can. Calm down. I know it's hell. But that's what's going to buy the sympathy that makes your story worth all the money you can use for the rest of your life."

"I don't want the money. I want out."

Grant wet his lips with his tongue. "Erika . . . You can't *get* out. I can't get you out. Face it. You did kill Len. The only way you can get out is by the trial and acquittal."

"Months . . ." she sobbed.

"Followed by the whole rest of your life, living at ease, with security and comfort. It's what we agreed to. You can't lose your nerve. You don't dare."

"Do you *promise* me I'm going to be acquitted?"

"I promise you. Listen, I've been working. You let that desk clerk have a good look at you, so he'd be a witness for the prosecution. Well, he's not going to be any good now. In the first place, he sold his story. Then yesterday he told a private investigator of mine that he wasn't so very sure after all that the woman he saw was you. My guy got that on tape. If they use him as a witness—"

"Too much depends on Sonya and Freddy."

"Columbo interviewed both of them. They did alright. They'll be okay. When you add to that that they've got no witness that puts you at the scene, they've got no gun, they've got no fingerprints—"

"Has anyone said anything about the money Len gave me?"

Grant shook his head. "We'll call it a loan. You asked him for a loan. He was, after all, the father of your child. He felt sorry for you and gave you the money. You called him on the phone and asked for it, and he told you to stop by the house on Thursday evenings when his wife would be out playing bridge. He gave you the money in cash because he didn't want her to see canceled checks."

Erika nodded. "Okay. I'll stick to that story. No matter what."

2

7:49 P.M.

Columbo glanced around the Pacific Club. He had come in with Adrienne, and he grinned at her and said, "This sure is some elegant place. My! More like where you'd expect to find a man like Grant Kellogg. I mean, to find him here instead of in a bowling-alley bar".

"Speaking of whom, guess who's sitting at the bar. Is that Grant Kellogg, or is that Grant Kellogg?"

"Not a coincidence," said Columbo. "The young woman who works in his office said this was where he was going."

"You going to talk to him?"

"If he'll talk to me."

"I'll go on into the dining room," she said. "Dan's waiting for me. I appreciate your time."

"Well, we were comin' to the same place."

"Riding in that car of yours is an adventure I never want to miss."

"Well, you don't often see real leather seats in cars anymore."

She laughed. "Okay, Columbo. I'll respect your confidence."

Columbo walked over to the bar. Grant Kellogg was sipping from a martini on the rocks. He wore a handsome double-breasted blue blazer, with gray slacks. Columbo's collar was unbuttoned, and it seemed appropriate to pull up the knot of his tie. Adrienne had insisted he must check his raincoat. He slapped cigar ash off the lapel of his gray suit.

"Mr. Kellogg," he said. "I hope I'm not intruding on your privacy."

"Lieutenant Columbo. Sit down. Whether you're intruding on my privacy depends on whether you've come here to interrogate me."

"Oh, no, Sir. Nothin' like that. I'm taking the evening off, so to speak." He paused and stared for a moment at Emily, the topless barmaid. "Uh . . . Mrs. Columbo's gone out to a movie she wanted to see, with some of her friends. I didn't really want to see it, so—"

"I didn't realize you were a member here."

"I'm not, really. I came in as a guest of somebody who is. Miss Adrienne Boswell. Of course, y' know, when I show my gold shield I can get in anywhere. I try not to take advantage of that."

"Let me buy you a drink. What'll you have?"

"Oh, uh, Scotch and soda. A light one. It's very kind of you, Sir."

Grant nodded at Emily. Columbo was conscious that he was staring at the girl. "What kind of Scotch would you like, Sir?" she asked.

"Oh, uh . . . Cutty would be fine."

"Hold it. Pour Lieutenant Columbo a Glenfiddich," said Grant.

"Lieutenant Columbo!" Emily glanced back and forth between the two men. "Oh, *my!*"

"He's going to give me the third-degree tonight, Emily. He's the best homicide detective in Los Angeles, and I'm more than a little afraid."

The girl laughed and turned to the shelf behind the bar to take down the bottle of single-malt Scotch.

"I notice that you've checked out my alibi witnesses."

"Well, yes, Sir. I have to do that."

Grant nodded. "I realize that only two of them can testify with certainty to the precise time when Erika arrived at Ten Strikes. The others are certain they saw her there, but aren't as certain of the exact time."

"Yes, Sir."

"Since the defense and prosecution have to exchange information, I can tell you that your motel clerk has changed his story. Now he's not sure he saw Erika that night. He says he could have been wrong."

"He was sure when he talked to me," said Columbo. "He

didn't have any doubt when that newspaper reporter interviewed him."

"That's because he was paid for his story. It wouldn't have been worth anything if he'd said he wasn't certain."

"What I'd like to know," said Columbo, "is how that reporter, Miss Mahoney, knew about Logan. He called in and asked to talk to the detective in charge of the Wylie murder investigation, and I went out and talked to him. *I* didn't tell anybody about that. But she—"

"It's simple enough, Columbo. Don't be naïve—as if I thought you were. The boy decided that here was a chance to pick up some money. I bet that newspaper paid him thousands of dollars for that interview."

Emily put a double Scotch on the bar, in a separate glass. She served the soda and ice on the side.

Columbo tasted the Scotch. "My! That's *special!* That's sure some whiskey."

"Erika's very unhappy in jail," said Grant. "She's pressing me hard to get the case docketed and tried."

"She's not the kind of person you expect to find in jail."

"No, she's not. Erika's a fine woman, one who's suffered some misfortunes in her life. It's tough being a woman whose only claim on the world, her only way of making it in this world, is that she's exceptionally attractive."

"There's something I'm gonna have to ask sooner or later, Mr. Kellogg. You may not want to answer. Was Mr. Wylie giving money to Miss Björling?"

"Why do you ask?"

"Well, she deposited cash in November and January—two thousand dollars, then five thousand. Each time, that came just one day after Mr. Wylie withdrew the same amount from his financial-management account. I just wondered if—"

"Yes, Lieutenant. Loans. Erika needed the money.

Badly. She's been out of work a long time. Len—which was his real name, you know—let her have two loans. He felt sorry for her."

"Why cash, Sir, if you know?"

"He didn't want his wife to find out he was giving Erika money. He had her come to the house and pick it up on Thursday evenings, when his wife would be out playing bridge."

"Both times? Thursday evenings?"

"I told you, Columbo. That's when his wife would be away from the house."

"For sure?"

Grant's face hardened. "I said it. That's when Faye would be away from the house."

"Well, it's very curious. I, uh—" Columbo shook his head. "Little inconsistencies bother me."

"What inconsistency?"

"Well, Sir, y' see. Mr. Wylie withdrew five thousand dollars from his account on January 9, which was a Monday; and Miss Björling deposited five thousand dollars in cash on January eleventh, which was Wednesday. And in November, he withdrew money on Friday, November fourth. She deposited the same amount in cash on Monday, the seventh."

Grant Kellogg grinned and shook his head. "I don't know what the answer is, Lieutenant. But you're right when you call it a little inconsistency. I'll ask Erika about it. Maybe her memory isn't one hundred percent accurate. You understand, she's emotionally distressed."

"Yeah, that's prob'ly the reason. She's upset. Anyway, I didn't mean to cross-examine you. Sorry. This is really good Scotch. I gotta write down the name of it."

TWENTY-TWO

1

Sunday, April 23—10:22 A.M.

Sunday morning he went shopping for a new raincoat. Mrs. Columbo insisted he must. Because he wanted to go alone and not have her pressing him to buy, he slipped away while she was out shopping for the groceries she would need to make the lasagna she was serving to him and their guests for dinner.

He went to an outlet store where he figured he could look and not have to talk to a salesman. It didn't work that way. They had a steel rack of raincoats, and no sooner had he begun to look than a salesman—a young fellow with bristly hair, wearing a loud checked jacket and a maroon satin necktie—sidled up to him and offered his assistance.

"A new raincoat, Sir? We've got some dandies. Some of them on sale. This week only."

"Well, I'm just lookin'," Columbo said.

"That one you're wearing is a veteran. I bet you've had good service out of that, for a lot of years."

"Good service? I mean to tell ya it's given me good service. You wouldn't believe."

"How about a style like this?" The young man pulled a raincoat from the rack. "Handsome, don't you think? Why don't you try it on, just for size?"

"Well, I—"

"Let me help you." The young salesman helped him out of his raincoat and laid it over the rack. "Now try this one. It's a lighter color, as you can see, and—"

"I don't know. This color's gonna show dirt a lot."

"Maybe a black coat?"

"And I need a lot of room in the pockets. Y' see, I'm a policeman, homicide investigator, and I carry a lot of stuff in my pockets."

"Then try *this* one. It's very stylish and has big pockets. And, I don't know . . . This coat just *says* policeman. I mean, it just *says* authority and—"

"Yeah, but the first thing that'd happen, I'd lose the belt. I'm untidy. I . . . I tell ya, I'm just lookin'. I really shouldn't take your time."

The young man stared disdainfully at the stained and tattered raincoat he had put on top of the rack. "You do need a new coat, Sir."

"Maybe. But it's like you said, that one has given me a lot of service. I figure it's got more in it. I just thought I'd look. My wife sent me."

"Well . . . If I can help you further, I'll be over there. Just let me know."

2

It was good to have Sunday off, and a nice afternoon nap would have suited. Huh-uh. Mrs. Columbo had a better idea. He should go to the beach, so he'd be out of the house while she was cooking. Okay, it might have been relaxing, except that Mrs. C. insisted she would send along a picnic lunch so he could stay three or four hours, instead of the one early-morning hour he liked to spend with Dog.

Worse than that, she insisted he must wear swimming trunks and actually venture into the water. He did, for about five minutes; but he couldn't swim and couldn't imagine why anyone would want to, unless he were in the navy. Besides, he sunburned easily and painfully. What was more, the splashing of the waves threatened to douse his cigar. Also, he figured he was a comic spectacle on the beach: a middle-aged guy with something of a paunch, wearing out-of-style boxer trunks and trying to keep his stub of cigar alight—in contrast to the California beach types, all handsome and sleek and in love with sun and sand and water. Except for walking Dog early in the morning, he just wasn't a beach guy.

Back home in late afternoon, he took the Beretta off the shelf in the hall closet and checked it for rust. It wasn't rusting. He wrapped it carefully in a towel and put it back. The revolver he'd kept in the closet for many years had been a simple, straightforward weapon. He had understood how it worked. The works of this pistol were hidden inside it. You couldn't even look at it and tell if it was loaded. Columbo figured the thing was dangerous.

He worked a little on his car, washing it and rubbing down the leather upholstery. There was something a man could find satisfaction in: taking good care of his car.

Then he had to take a shower and dress for dinner. Not only that, he had to slap aftershave on his face. He had to serve drinks and open the wine. And try to keep the conversation off the Erika Björling case.

About 9:30 he excused himself from the party for a few minutes and went to his den. He switched his telephone answering machine to record the two calls he was about to make.

The first number he dialed answered on the second ring.

——"Hello."

——"Hi. Is Dana home?"

——"There's no Dana here. You must have the wrong number."

——"Oh, sorry. Isn't this 531–2974?"

——"No, it isn't."

——"Well, I'm calling long distance, you see, and I don't want to dial the same wrong number twice."

——"I'm afraid that's your problem. You've called a wrong number. Okay?"

——"I'm sorry to have bothered you. It's an imposition to get a wrong-number call on Sunday evening."

——"Okay. But please don't dial the same number again."

She hung up.

He dialed a second number.

——"This is the law offices of Grant Kellogg. Neither I nor any member of my staff are here right now. Our office hours are from 8:30 to 5:00, Monday through Saturday. If you would like to leave a message, please wait for the beep and then be sure to give your name and number so we can return your call. Thank you for calling."

3

Captain Sczciegel had left word for Columbo to come to his office. The captain was grinning broadly when Columbo came in.

"Have a nice day off, Columbo?"

"Super. Oh, yes, Sir. Very nice. And you?"

"I don't suppose you took any time to carry your Beretta out to the range and get in some practice? No, don't tell me. I don't even want to know. Look at this."

He handed Columbo a copy of *PROBE*. The headline on the front page was—

ERIKA BJÖRLING TOPLESS!
ACCUSED MURDERESS AS YOU'VE NEVER SEEN HER!

What was promised on the front page filled page three: five photographs of Erika Björling with her breasts bare. They were beach pictures, maybe taken somewhere like St. Tropez. She was topless, but she wasn't flaunting it.

"It's a bunch of crap, Columbo. As you know. But it adds to the pressure on us. Dunedin has been on the phone already, wanting to know if we've got the evidence that wraps up the case. Do we?"

Columbo shook his head. "Mr. Dunedin knows very well. With what we've got, it's a touch-and-go case. The alibi witnesses that put her in the bar at the Ten Strikes bowling alley at the time of the murder are coming unglued, little by little; but they're still better witnesses than any we've got that puts her in Bel Air at the time of the killing."

"What's wrong with the alibi witnesses? Have you filled Dunedin in on this?"

"Haven't got it nailed down yet, Cap'n. But Fred Mansfield needs money awful bad. Also, Sonya Pavlov spent the small hours of Friday-Saturday night in Mr. Kellogg's apartment. When I got the facts, I'll give 'em to the DA."

Sczciegel grinned. "Spent the night—? Columbo, you're—" He shook his head. "I won't even ask how you figured that one out."

4

10:23 A.M.

Columbo sat on an orange fiberglass chair in an office at Sybil Brand Institute. He'd taken a cigar from his raincoat pocket, then realized the rule forbade smoking. He had brought with him a copy of *PROBE*, and it lay on the table before him. He read some of the stories—about appearances by Satan in West Texas, in which the demon corrupted young people by compelling them to listen to endless hours of rock-and-roll music; of a creature from outer space who had carried a Mississippi woman to another galaxy and returned her, after his race had subjected her to an exhaustive physical and mental examination and then displayed her naked in a zoo for a week; of a woman who had spotted a slender and youthful Elvis in a supermarket and persuaded him to acknowledge that he was indeed Elvis Presley but swore her not to reveal that he was about to announce a concert tour . . .

"Lieutenant Columbo?"

"Yes, Ma'am. You're Margaret Phillips?"

"That's me." The woman sat down. She was an attractive blond, maybe forty years old, in the uniform of a guard. "They said you wanted to see me."

"Yes, Ma'am."

"Lieutenant . . . The inmates in here are supposed to call me 'ma'am.' I'd just as soon you didn't. I'm Peg."

He grinned and nodded. "Okay. It's a habit. You're not the first woman to tell me not to call her that. Anyway, you may or may not be able to help me a little. It's an off chance." He shrugged. "If it works— Anyway, have you seen this?"

He handed her the tabloid, and she turned immediately to page three. She smiled and shook her head.

"Is that her?" he asked. "Are those really pictures of Miss Björling?"

Peg Phillips turned up her hands. "How could I tell? Pictures . . . "

"Well, you might be able to. Y' see, I asked for whoever had put Miss Björling through a strip search, once or more than once. You might have seen something—like a birthmark, a mole, or a scar—that would tell you whether or not those pictures are really of Miss Björling."

"You think maybe they're not? And is it important? Has it got to do with—?"

"Well— There's something very strange about her case. Her lawyer is selling her story for every dollar he can get out of it. Which may not mean anything but that he's mercenary, and so's she. Or maybe it *does* mean somethin'. I wondered if you'd see anything about those pictures that might tell you the body is not hers."

"Faked, you mean?"

Columbo shrugged. "Could be."

The jail guard frowned over the pictures. She hesitated for a long moment. "Well . . . You may have a point.

Uh . . . Miss Björling doesn't have any scars or birthmarks or moles. But she's got—"

"I know this is embarrassing," Columbo suggested.

"Not for *me* it isn't. But— Would I ever have to testify to this?"

"No. Just for information."

Peg Phillips shook her head. "*Not* her body. Her head on the body of another woman, a model. Look. Her nipples. Little bitty wrinkled fellas, with dark buds that stand up. Erika Björling's are big and smooth and shiny. No buds. I mean— Hell, I've seen 'em four or five times. We do strip-search prisoners. We have to, y' know. You wouldn't *believe* what they try to bring in, and where they try to hide stuff."

"This has been very helpful. I can't tell ya how helpful."

"Anytime, Lieutenant."

5

12:11 P.M.

Columbo and Adrienne had picked up hot dogs from a cart vendor and walked out on a pier. The wind was picking up, and the sea was restless.

"I love to look at the ocean," he said.

"You and Dan would like each other. *He* loves to look at the ocean."

"I like lookin' at it better than touchin' it."

Adrienne laughed. "That's how I am about snow. I like to look at it; it's beautiful; but don't ask me to go skiing. Even Dan wants me to go skiing. No way."

She was dressed casually again, in tight, faded jeans and a sweatshirt. She enjoyed her hot dog. She enjoyed oysters on the half shell, and caviar, but she relished a cart-boiled hot dog smeared with yellow mustard.

"Need some information," said Columbo.

"Here I thought you invited me for a romantic lunch be-cause—"

"Adrienne . . . Serious. I got something interesting. I'll tell you what it is, but you can't use it. Okay?"

"I never violated your trust before, did I?"

"You sure didn't. Well . . . Look. Those pictures of Erika Björling, in *PROBE*. They're fakes. I mean, for sure. That's not her. That's her face on some other woman's body. Don't ask me how I know."

"God, I wouldn't *want* to know!"

"The point is, that newspaper prob'ly paid good money for those. And other good money for the Logan interview. I wonder what the top dog at *PROBE* would think—might maybe *do*—if he found out he'd been snookered."

Adrienne smiled slyly. "The point is, how do we let him know?"

"I was thinkin' about that. I figured you prob'ly know who's the publisher."

6

1:45 P.M.

Standing at the big window in Adrienne's living room, Columbo stared at the enviable view she had of the coast and the Pacific. He had her portable telephone in his hand and listened to her as she called an office in New York.

It was not easy for anyone to get through on the tele-phone to Harry Gottsman, the reclusive publisher of *PROBE,* but her name cut through some levels of corporate bureaucracy, and finally the notorious publisher of the scandal-sheet tabloid came on the line.

"Gottsman speaking."

"I guess I don't need to introduce myself, Mr. Gottsman. You wouldn't have taken my call if you didn't recognize my name."

"I've heard your name, Miss Boswell. Interested in coming to work for me?"

Adrienne chuckled. "I think I'll pass up that privilege for the moment. On the other hand, if it's an offer, I'll keep it in mind."

"Anytime. Listen. Tell me what you're making, and I'll better it."

"That's an intriguing proposition, Mr. Gottsman."

"I bet you got a different proposition in mind. Why'd you call? If I'm not being too blunt."

"You've been snookered. I thought you might like to know. I thought maybe also, if I tell you how you've been snookered, you might be willing to share a bit of information with me."

"Journalistic courtesy," said Gottsman, a barely subdued laugh in his voice.

"We got a deal?"

"Tell me how I've been snookered."

"Your pictures of the topless Erika Björling. Doctored photos. Her face. Not her body."

A silence followed.

"Got me, Mr. Gottsman? I can prove it."

"How can you prove it?" His voice had hardened. Adrienne winked at Columbo, who had come into her office with the wireless telephone and was watching as well as listening. "How can you? And what you plan to do about it?"

"What I plan to do about it is nothing. I'm giving you

information. You give me some. We never talked to each other."

"All right. What you want to know from me?"

"Who tipped you that Logan claims he saw Erika Björling in his motel the night of the Wylie murder. Incidentally, he's backing off on that story. He told an assistant district attorney he could have been wrong."

"Backing— Alright. How do you know the pictures are fake?"

"Don't ask me for more, but the tip comes from somebody who's seen the beauteous Erika in the altogether more than once, and swears that's not her body. It seems, Mr. Gottsman, that she has certain specific bodily characteristics that are not matched in the photographs."

Again, a silence on the line. Then— "You say you don't plan to tip this?"

"What good would that do me? It's okay with me if you run pictures of the semi-nude Erika Björling. What I want to know is, who told you Logan would claim she was at the King's Court Motel the night of the murder?"

"Who the hell do you think?" Gottsman asked. "The same son of a bitch who sold me fake pictures!"

"And that person is?"

"*Grant Kellogg!*"

TWENTY-THREE

1

Tuesday, April 25—9:43 A.M.

Personnel of Sybil Brand Institute stood behind the lights and cameras and watched the drama being taped for television. The prisoners in four cells in the reception area had been moved to a holding pen, as if they were on their way to court. One cell had been swept of all litter, and the graffiti had been scrubbed from its walls. A prisoner who had served in the United States Marine Corps had earned extra television privileges by making up the cot in the tight, determinedly neat military manner. Two cameras sat on pedestals, Lights stood on tripods. Microphones in dishes were aimed at the cell.

When everything was ready, Erika was brought in and locked in the cell—locked lest she accidentally shove the door open while she was being interviewed. She wore blue dungarees and white rubber-and-canvas shoes. She had applied a little pale-pink lipstick and submitted to a dusting with powder and a little penciling of her eyebrows.

The director was a hyperactive young man with a yellow mustache. "Okay," he said to Erika. "You're a pro. I don't have to tell you how to do it. Don't shift your eyes. The audience can't be allowed to guess that you're taking any direction. When I want to give you a signal, I'll step behind Veronica, so it will look like you're keeping your eyes on her."

Veronica Drake was the interviewer. She was a striking woman with spray-sculptured hair, glossy brushed-on lip color, and intense blue eyes. She was wearing a dark-blue dress with gleaming brass buttons and a skirt three inches above her knees. The preliminaries had been taped earlier, or would be taped later, and she began simply by walking up to the cell door and saying—

"This cell, nine feet long by six feet wide, is the present home of glamorous television personality Erika Björling. She has agreed to an exclusive jail interview with *American Chronicle,* and the Los Angeles women's prison, the Sybil Brand Institute, has also extended its gracious cooperation. Erika . . . good evening."

Erika rose from the cot and stepped over to the bars.

"Let's get something out of the way first," said Veronica Drake. "Did you kill Tim Wylie?"

Erika shook her head. "No," she said firmly. "Absolutely not."

"Then being in here has to be a terrible ordeal for you."

Erika gripped a steel bar in her left hand and with her right wiped a tear from her cheek. "Yes. It's unbelievably horrible."

"You're not saying that the personnel of this jail treat you cruelly?"

"Oh, no. They just do their jobs. In fact, they've been kind to me. But they can't let me out."

The interview went on like that for about ten minutes.

Erika wept and talked about the agony of confinement. Prompted by Veronica Drake, she described a strip-search, told how it felt to be handcuffed, talked about the meals she ate, talked about her job sorting laundry, described the panic she felt each time she woke in the night and remembered she was locked in. She ended the interview by saying she would rather die than be convicted and face the prospect of life in prison.

American Chronicle paid one million dollars for that interview. It would be broadcast the next evening.

2

10:18 A.M.

Columbo rapped on the glass with a quarter. He rapped again. Then again. When he was about to give up and leave, a man emerged from somewhere inside the closed bowling alley and came to the door. He shook his head and pointed at the sign saying the place was closed. Columbo showed his shield.

The man unlocked and opened the door.

"Columbo, Sir. Lieutenant Columbo, LAPD Homicide. You are—?"

"Hupp. Mace Hupp. I own this place."

"Yes, Sir. You're the man I came to see. Can I come in?"

The man shrugged and pushed the door wide open. He was a man of fifty years, as Columbo judged. He judged also that not many years ago, this Mace Hupp—whose name was Mason Hupp, actually—had been a handsome man and a lady-killer. Now he had an interesting, engaging face marred only by prominent teeth that needed a dentist's attention. His dark hair was turning gray. He smiled. The smile was one of genuine amusement, but also of total cynicism. He was a man who had seen something of the world and maybe didn't like it too much.

Jesús Ruiz had done a background check on Hupp and reported that he did not actually own Ten Strikes. It was owned by a corporation that employed him as a front man. He was a bowler and pool player with enough of a name to attract customers to the big alley.

"Sure. C'mon in. You're investigatin' the Wylie murder, right? I don't know the first thing about it."

Columbo looked around. Ten Strikes was a much bigger place than he'd thought, since his attention before had been focused exclusively on the lounge. There were twenty alleys.

Hupp noticed him staring at the alleys. "You bowl, Lieutenant? A lot of guys from the Department do. I get a lot of cops come in and bowl."

"No. Mrs. Columbo bowls. She's a member of a ladies' league. My game is pool."

"Really? Y' shoot good?"

"Decent."

Hupp grinned. "Come over here. I got six tables. Do a little pool business on the side."

He showed Columbo into a room where indeed six pool tables stood. He switched on the lights.

"My. This is a first-class—"

Hupp racked balls on the first table. "Nine-ball, Lieutenant?"

"That's my game."

"Go ahead and break. Ten dollars?"

"Make it one," said Columbo. "On a policeman's salary, that's more the style."

"Dollar it is. Break."

Columbo broke the rack and sank the four. He sank the

one but missed the two. Hupp bent over the table and smoothly ran the remaining balls. He broke then, made the seven on the break, and again ran out the game.

Columbo grinned, put his two dollars on the table, and shook his head. "I know when I'm overmatched," he said.

Hupp shoved his two dollars back toward him. "I should've told you, Lieutenant. I was California state champion four straight years. Came in third in one national competition, fifth another time. I'd have liked to run the biggest poolroom in Los Angeles, but there's more to be made with bowling. Keep on shootin'. But no money."

Columbo pushed the two one-dollar bills back to Hupp. "Worth it to see you play," he said.

Hupp racked the balls again and motioned to Columbo to break. "I bet you got somethin' in mind. You didn't come in to play a couple racks of pool."

Columbo nodded. "I guess the two alibi witnesses that work here work for you."

"Right."

"Y' know anything about them that I ought to know?"

Hupp shook his head. "Sonya's a good girl. She hired Freddy. I don't know anything about him. She says he's okay, he's okay with me. For a little while I was afraid Sonya was turnin' tricks—which I couldn't tolerate—but then I figured out that she wasn't. She plays the main chance. She has to."

"Meanin'?"

"Short of money. She's got a son that's a wonderful kid. She wants to send him to college, but she can't afford it. She'd *turn* tricks if that would get that boy a university education. I'd lend her the money, but—" Hupp shrugged. "We all got our problems."

"Well . . . It's been great to meet ya. When I got time, I'll come in and let you give me some more pool lessons."

"Y' ever play straight pool, Lieutenant? Fifty-ball? Hundred-ball? Nine-ball's for television and gamblers. And it's sickening to watch guys come in and shoot eight-ball, which is for children. Straight pool. Call your shot. *That's* pool."

Columbo nodded. "I love that. Hardly ever have time for it."

"You come in mornings before I'm open, and we'll make time for it."

"You think I won't? I will. I'll be in to play. I'll call. And, hey, how'd you like to play with a gorgeous red-headed gal that beats me regularly?"

"Bring her, Columbo. I'd love to give *her* lessons."

Columbo laughed and moved toward the door. "Oh, say. There is one more thing I ought to ask ya. Little thing. It must be good for business to have celebrities like Erika Björling and Grant Kellogg come in. Miss Pavlov always points 'em out to customers, I understand. That attract customers for ya?"

Hupp shrugged. "I never saw Erika Björling here. I understand she came in once or twice before she was arrested. I go in the lounge every half hour or so, to see how it's going. I never saw her. I did see Kellogg a coupla times. Off the record, he and Sonya— Well. But Erika Björling?" He turned down the corners of his mouth and shook his head. "She never attracted any business here. If she came in at all, it was once or twice. That's all."

3

11:26 A.M.

"Hiya," said Columbo as he walked into the service bay of an automobile agency in Long Beach. "You Gus

Schmidt? My name's Columbo." He showed his shield. "LAPD homicide."

The mechanic ducked out from under the Toyota he had up on a rack, and grabbed a rag to wipe his hands before he shook hands with Columbo. "What can I do for you?" He was a tall man, slender almost to the point of emaciation, with a long, pointed chin, a pointed nose, and cheeks sunken under prominent cheekbones. But he had jolly, dancing eyes.

Columbo looked up at the car on the rack. "You service Peugeots?"

"I'll service a baleen whale if I can get the parts."

Columbo grinned. "There y' go! Well . . . my car doesn't need any service right now. But I'll keep ya in mind. Uh—What I came in to talk about is a murder case I'm investigating."

"The Erika Björling case."

"Right."

"I saw her in the lounge at the Ten Strikes Alley the night of the murder."

"What time?"

"Ten maybe. Ten-fifteen."

"Y' ever see her there before?"

"Nope. I bowl once a week—member of a league, y' understand. I never saw her there before. But— I might not."

"You and Mike Reilly are members of the same league?"

"Right. Sure."

"Well, now. You say you saw Erika Björling at ten o'clock or so. Mike thinks he saw her about nine. When did you guys finish your game that night?"

Schmidt stiffened. "Hey. Is Mike in some kind of trouble?"

"No, no, no, no. I'm just tryin' to compare notes, y' understand. If Mike says it was nine, you say it was ten—

Big deal. But it's the kind of thing I gotta check into, y' know. It's just a question of judgment. I don't think Mike messed around with the facts. Nothin' like."

The mechanic's cheeks swelled out as he blew away a big breath and frowned. "Hey. We start bowling sometime after eight. You know, we all got jobs, then eat supper with the wife and kids, and— Gotta drive to the alley. Wives are always on our butts about what time we get home after— which is always close to eleven. Got finished and went in for a beer and saw Erika Björling by nine?" He shook his head. "No way!"

Columbo nodded. "That's helpful. I 'preciate it."

Schmidt grinned. "Hey. Don't lock that luscious dish up for the rest of her life. What a waste!"

"I'll keep that in mind."

TWENTY-FOUR

1

Tuesday, April 25—1:01 P.M.

"Hiya, Mobley. Sorry I didn't get back to you sooner," Columbo said to the man in the police forensic lab. "Whatta ya figure? Anything?"

"It may be interesting, Columbo. None of the samples are as long as I'd like to have, but they're long enough to suggest an identification."

"Good."

"Listen, I'd like to call Sergeant Maria Prieta in here to talk to you. She's been a big help."

"Call her."

Lieutenant Roger Mobley put in the call. Columbo sat and stared around the room, at the varied electronic equipment that covered the tables and shelves. All kinds of tests were run here, some of them mysterious to him.

"She'll be here in a minute," Mobley said. "Will it be possible to get more extensive samples, you think?"

"It may be, if it comes to it. Right now, if it *suggests*

somethin', that may be good enough. I got an idea, and I'm looking to reinforce it."

Sergeant Prieta arrived. She was a young woman apparently of mixed African and Indian descent, with flawlessly smooth chocolaty skin, close-cropped, charcoal-black hair, and piercing dark eyes.

"Let's listen to the Erika Björling tape one more time, "Mobley suggested."

He pressed a button on a small tape player. Loaded in it was the cartridge from the telephone answering machine in Erika's apartment in Van Nuys.

—"Thursday, April 13, seven . . . p.m." "Hi, Erika. This is Constanza. Give me a call when you can, okay? Kinda anxious to hear from you. Hoping we can work something out."

—"Thursday, April 13, seven . . . twenty-two p.m." "Miss Björling? This is Larry calling again. I don't wanta be a nuisance, but I'd really appreciate a yes or no answer. If it's no, it's no. But I would like to have an answer. I mean . . . you can tell me to go to hell if you want to. That'd be better than no call from you at all."

—"Thursday, April 13, seven . . . thirty-eight p.m." "Constanza again. Guess you're out for the evening. I'll try you again tomorrow, okay?"

Sergeant Prieta grinned. "Constanza speaks with a fake accent. That's like Benny Hill pretending he's a flamenco dancer. Not Spanish. No way Spanish, not any dialect."

"Did you listen to the other answering-machine tapes?" Columbo asked.

"Yes." But she shrugged.

"Okay, the voiceprints," Mobley said. "Like I said, we really need better samples. But— The woman who answered her phone Sunday night and talked with the guy about his wrong number— Columbo! You're no better at faking than the man and woman on the answering-machine tapes. If you ever talked to that woman—"

"I thought that wasn't a half-bad southern accent," said Columbo.

"Anyway, the woman you talked to is very likely the same woman who faked the Spanish accent on Erika Björling's answering machine. Look."

He played the Sunday-night conversation, sending the sound into an oscilloscope as well as into a speaker. The glowing green phosphor on the face of the tube formed a distinctive jagged pattern.

"Now," said Mobley. He laid out photographs taken of the screen. "This is the word 'okay,' spoken twice Sunday night. "You can see the two 'okays' make identical patterns. And here are two 'okays' off the Björling answering-machine tape. *They* are identical. Then we try to match all four. You can see they are not identical, but they are very, very similar."

Columbo clapped his hands together. "That means 'Constanza' is Sonya Pavlov."

"Not beyond a reasonable doubt," Mobley said dryly. "Now— 'Larry' uses the words 'call' and 'calling.' Kellogg uses those words on his answering-machine's outgoing message. The voice prints are not identical, but I'd guess that 'Larry' is Grant Kellogg."

"Bingo!"

Sergeant Prieta frowned. "Why would he take a risk like that?"

Columbo shrugged. "I don't know, but I'll guess. He didn't want any more people involved. If he did what I'm beginning to suspect he did, he had too many people in on it already."

2

"Do you fully understand what you're saying, Lieutenant Columbo?" asked Charles Dunedin, the Assistant District Attorney. Columbo and Captain Sczciegel sat in chairs facing the young lawyer's desk. "You're suggesting that Erika Björling's defense attorney is potentially a co-defendant."

"I can only go where the evidence leads me, Sir."

"Can you suggest a *reason* why Grant Kellogg himself would put a fake message on her answering machine?"

"Yes, Sir. It's only a guess, you understand, and I gotta have lots more evidence before I'd call it a fact, but I'm guessing Mr. Kellogg *wanted* Miss Björling to be arrested and charged with murder."

"Now, wait a minute. Why would the woman's defense lawyer want—"

" 'Cause he's made more than a million dollars already out of selling her story, and there's lots more millions where the first one came from."

Dunedin shook his head. "It's preposterous, Lieutenant. I mean, c'mon!"

"Columbo has reasons to think what he's suggesting," said Sczciegel.

"I'd like to hear them."

"Okay," said Columbo. "What evidence do we have against her? First, there's the evidence of the note. Mr. Kellogg said she wrote it in February, but a chemical test of the ballpoint ink proves it was written within a week before the murder. Second, when I went to arrest her, she said she'd been at home until after eight, but there were three unanswered calls on her telephone answering machine. The voiceprints suggest those calls were made by Mr. Kellogg and Miss Pavlov—who is, of course, the chief alibi witness. Those calls were put on that recorder to make it look like Miss Björling was lying and, together with the note, make me decide to arrest her. Then, when she went out to the Wylie home in Bel Air—*if* she went to the Wylie home in Bel Air—she didn't go directly but checked into a motel, where she made sure to let the room clerk have a good look at her. So we had a witness to testify she was within ten minutes drive of the Wylie house at 8:40 or so. But that witness turned sour for us when he sold his story to a tabloid. Where did the tabloid get his name? From Grant Kellogg."

"This doesn't make a grain of sense," argued Dunedin, flushing and shaking his head.

"It doesn't make sense until you look at it this way," said Columbo. "They *built* a case against her, strong enough to make us arrest and charge her. Then they built a defense case, strong enough to make sure she'd be acquitted— based on alibi witnesses. While she's in jail, the celebrated Erika Björling, whose face and figure is known to everybody in America, Mr. Kellogg hires an agent, gets in touch with a tabloid publisher, auctions off a television interview . . . Let me tell ya something else, Sir. You saw the topless pictures of Miss Björling in *PROBE?* They're fakes. It's her face put on another woman's body. The publisher of *PROBE* is very upset about that."

Charles Dunedin closed his eyes and shook his head. "You can't make it stick," he said quietly. "I'm beginning to believe you, but *we* can't make it stick."

"No, Sir. We gotta figure some *way* to make it stick."

Columbo rang the bell at the house on North Perugia Way. Vicky Glassman opened the door.

"Am I early?"

"You said a quarter to five."

"I have a way of showing up places early. Sometimes it embarrasses people. Sometimes it embarrasses me."

"Well . . . Come on in. For once you need that raincoat. Mother's in the living room."

Faye sat on the couch. A figure still marked by tragedy, she had recovered her color, was wearing a little makeup, and sat erect, not slumped, wearing a red silk ao dai. "Lieutenant Columbo," she said, "I hope you're not surprised to see that I've redecorated a bit. I could hardly have left that blood-soaked carpet on the floor, could I?"

"No, Ma'am."

The fake art had been taken down and replaced with framed lithographs: posters by early-twentieth-century artists.

"The girls will be playing bridge here Thursday night," said Faye. "They can't wait to see this room again," she added dryly. "I'm ready to answer their questions now, to say things like, 'Oh, yes, right there is where he was.' "

"Mother!"

Faye shrugged. "I'm going to sell the place and move into a nice condo with a view of the ocean. Why not?"

Vicky flushed. The idea of selling her family home did not appeal to her, apparently. She was wearing tennis whites, with fluffy pompoms on her shoes. She had not sat down but was standing at the bar. "What's yours, Lieutenant?"

"Just a very light Scotch and soda. I gotta drive home, ya know."

"I bet you came out here with some kind of a question," Vicky said. "I'm beginning to understand you, Columbo. You don't do things without a reason."

"Well, I do have a question. A little thing that's started to bother me. I've been thinkin' about that note that Miss Björling wrote to Mr. Wylie. Y' know? Mr. Kellogg says she wrote it in February—"

"It wasn't in the drawer of the escritoire for two months, I can tell you," said Faye. "That's where we keep postage stamps, and I was in that drawer every three or four days."

"It wasn't in the escritoire, Ma'am. That's where the newspapers said it was, and I don't know where they got that idea. It was in the nightstand beside Mr. Wylie's bed."

Vicky handed her mother a drink—gin or vodka over ice; Columbo couldn't tell which.

"It wasn't in there for two months, either," said Faye. "I looked in that drawer every few days, too."

"Mother . . . why in the world—?"

"It was where he kept his stash of condoms. I looked in there from time to time, and not just out of curiosity; I thought I ought to know what he was up to. His escapades had cost too much money, and—"

"Do you mean to say he was *using* them?"

"Vicky, for god's sake!"

"You're certain about this?" Columbo asked.

Faye nodded firmly. "I counted his supply. I didn't just glance in casually. He kept those and a nasal inhaler and some tablets for acid stomach. No letter or note. If anything like that had been in there, I'd have seen it."

Columbo smiled. "The investigating officers took an inventory of what was in that drawer that night. It was just like you said: a dozen or so Ramses condoms, a Vicks nasal inhaler, and a package of Tums. And the note."

"There was no note there on, say, Monday or Tuesday," said Faye. "I know damn well there wasn't."

"This is very helpful, Ma'am. This is very helpful. Suddenly the whole thing makes sense."

4

8:11 P.M.

"It'd have been nice if *we'd* got to see that television interview," said Miriam.

Erika sat on her cot, her shoulders hunched, her eyes wet with tears. "Some things you don't get to do when you're in jail," she whispered.

"Ain't it a fact," Pearl muttered.

"The story is, you get a million dollars for that show," said Miriam.

"Yeah. I can use it to buy chewing gum and peanuts." Erika sighed. "A *billion* dollars wouldn't do me any good in here."

"Shit! You're gonna walk. You're gonna go. You'll get to spend your million dollars." Miriam stopped and grinned. "Or maybe you'll use it to buy your way out."

Erika got up and stepped to the bars of their cell, where Lily habitually stood, as if she could relate better to the world outside the imprisoning steel if she stood and folded her hands outside.

" 'Buy your way out . . . ' Hell, Miriam. You didn't have to do what got you in here. I . . . *did.*"

TWENTY-FIVE

1

Wednesday, April 26—10:11 A.M.

Grant Kellogg stirred sugar and heavy cream into his coffee. Columbo took his black.

"Am I wrong?" Grant asked. "Or do I have to suspect you are focusing some part of your investigation on *me?*"

"I just go where the facts lead me, Sir," Columbo said ingenuously.

"It would be highly unprofessional and improper for the police department to undertake an investigation into the personal life of an attorney for the defense. The court will never stand for it."

"Oh, I understand," Columbo agreed. "The personal life of the lawyers is no part of a case."

"Well, your patrol officers are not subtle, Lieutenant. Last night I get up to take a pee and see a black-and-white outside, shining a spotlight on a car in my driveway. Half an hour later, they're back. No spotlight this time, but— It ruined my night's sleep, Columbo. What were they doing?"

"I'd imagine looking for a stolen car."

Grant's face darkened and hardened. "Whose car?"

"I'm with Homicide, Mr. Kellogg, not Auto Theft."

"Okay. You're going to play it that way. You'd have no idea why I got an angry, threatening call from Harry Gottsman, would you?"

"Gottsman? I don't believe I know any Mr. Gottsman."

Grant drank coffee. He turned away from Columbo and looked out his window. "Is it any part of the investigation to know that Mary Nell Fiske is pregnant?"

"I didn't ask if she was. I was just runnin' the usual background check on your alibi witness, and—"

"You know how this is going to sound when it's heard before a court?"

"How what is going to sound, Mr. Kellogg?"

"You're running this so-called investigation far beyond any proper limit, Lieutenant Columbo. And you seem determined to pay no attention to obvious exculpatory facts. It may be that the van Gogh was a fake, but the burglars who came to steal it didn't know that. Why—?"

"Why did Mr. Wylie let the burglar in and serve him a drink?"

"Lieutenant, have you made any effort to find the burglar or burglars who stole the van Gogh, fake or not, and are the very likely murderer or murderers of Tim Wylie? I'll be asking you that in court."

"Mr. Kellogg— I gotta figure the best thing is for us to talk in the presence of Mr. Dunedin. Maybe in the presence of a judge. This thing has got beyond us just talkin' in private."

"Let's do it that way, Lieutenant. And on the record."

Thursday, April 27—1:08 P.M.

Word that some kind of hearing was being held had some-how leaked, and the hall outside the conference room was jammed with reporters and cameramen. Officers guarded the doors, and the principals entered the room through a rear door.

The District Attorney himself presided. Charles Dune-din would speak for the prosecution. Chief Wilson and Captain Sczciegel were present, but they would let Columbo speak. Erika sat beside Grant Kellogg, red-faced and tearful. She wore a white blouse and a black skirt and was handcuffed. Jesús Ruiz sat behind Columbo. A court stenographer recorded the proceedings.

Grant Kellogg spoke first. "Mr. District Attorney, I con-cede that this is a strictly informal hearing, but it is outra-geous that Miss Björling be kept handcuffed. I *demand* they be taken off her."

The District Attorney nodded. Erika grimaced as if it were painful as a woman unlocked and removed the hand-cuffs.

"I asked for this hearing," said Grant, "to put on record my emphatic protest against the unconscionable conduct of the Los Angeles Police Department, as represented by Lieutenant Columbo, in ignoring every scrap of evidence tending to exculpate my client, while focusing obsessively on weak evidence that tends to inculpate her, and con-ducting an irrational investigation directed at *me,* appar-ently because I dare to defend this unfortunate woman. I can only conclude that the Department is trying to bolster a weak case by attacking her counsel."

Charles Dunedin spoke. "Mr. Kellogg makes a dramatic speech, as always. Does he want to review the evidence at this time?"

"I most assuredly do," said Grant.

"That would be more appropriately done in court," said Dunedin, "but we have agreed to this hearing, with the understanding that the record made today can be shown to the court—*in camera* at least."

"Agreed," said Grant.

"Lieutenant Columbo," the District Attorney began.

"I don't know just how we're supposed to proceed here," said Columbo. "I thought Mr. Kellogg would probably want to ask me some questions. But, uh— Sir, would you be willing to *answer* some questions?"

"I do have some questions for you, Lieutenant, but I am not unwilling to answer any you may want to ask."

"Well, that's fine then. I thank ya. The first question— Well, let's see. Yesterday you mentioned a threatening call from a Mr. Gottsman. Would you mind telling us what that was about?"

"It's totally irrelevant."

Columbo turned to the District Attorney and shrugged.

"Mr. Kellogg," said the District Attorney, "it will be up to the judge, when he reviews this transcript, to decide what is relevant and irrelevant. If you intend to respond to all questions asked you by citing your personal opinion that the answer would be irrelevant, we might as well adjourn this hearing right now."

Grant frowned and pondered. "Alright. Harry Gottsman is unhappy about some photographs I sold him."

"What photographs are those, Sir?"

"The photographs showing the defendant semi-nude."

"I'd like to ask Miss Björling a question," said Columbo. "If that's okay. Miss Björling, have you seen the pictures we're talking about?"

Erika nodded. "Yes," she whispered.

"Well . . . Are those really pictures of you?"

She turned to Grant, and the two of them conferred hastily, in whispers.

Erika spoke to the District Attorney. "Do I have to answer?"

"You don't have to answer anything. You don't even have to be here. But the record of this hearing will be shown to the court—and maybe parts of it to the jury—and in any case it will become the basis for cross-examination."

She whispered to Grant again, then turned toward Columbo and said, "No."

"In other words, those were your face on somebody else's body."

"Yes."

"How much did Mr. Gottsman pay for those photos, Mr. Kellogg?"

"He paid $50,000, which I'm refunding. And what does that prove, Lieutenant?"

"Nothin'. Maybe nothin'. Another question. Who's Constanza, Miss Björling? You remember: the woman's voice on your answering machine."

"A girl who wanted to come to my apartment once a week to clean."

"What's her last name?"

"I don't know."

"How could you get in touch with her? Did you have her phone number?"

"No. I couldn't get in touch with her. She got in touch with me."

"And who's Larry?"

"Guy who wanted a date."

"What's *his* last name?"

"I don't know. I'd told him to quit calling me."

Columbo ran his hand through his already tousled hair. "Mr. Kellogg, I have somethin' to confess to you. I *did* have officers check your driveway Tuesday night. And Monday night. And last Friday night."

"That's what I'm complaining about," Grant snapped. "The Los Angeles Police Department is harassing me!"

"Well, Sir, I— I got a note here someplace. Lessee. Oh, yeah. Here it is. Uh . . . A car that's not yours parks in your driveway some nights. Friday night last week it showed up there about two o'clock and left around six on Saturday morning. That same car was there Monday night, about the same hours; and again, same car, same hours, Tuesday night. Whose car is that, Mr. Kellogg?"

"It's none of your business! Now, this *is* irrelevant. I *protest!"*

Columbo turned up the palms of his hands. "Really, I don't have to ask, Sir. We know whose car it is, from the license plates. It belongs to Miss Sonya Pavlov."

"Grant!" Erika shrieked.

3

2:01 P.M.

After a recess, taken to give Erika time to recover her composure and confer with her attorney, the hearing resumed.

Erika's face was red. The corners of her mouth turned down. She stared at the wall behind the District Attorney as if she saw nothing.

Grant Kellogg stared at Columbo. "What business is

it of yours if Miss Pavlov's car has been in my driveway?"

"She's your chief alibi witness, Sir."

Grant glowered.

"If you're conferring about her testimony between two and six in the morning, that's your business, Sir."

Erika sobbed.

"Lieutenant Columbo—"

The District Attorney interrupted. "Do you want to close this proceeding, Mr. Kellogg?"

Grant shook his head. "It's been turned into a travesty, but—"

"Can I ask another question of Miss Björling?"

Grant stared at Columbo. He sighed loudly. "Do your damnedest, Lieutenant," he said. "Nothing you've said amounts to the *slightest* evidence against my client."

Columbo scratched behind his ear. "Miss Björling, do you know what voiceprints are?"

Erika grabbed Grant's sleeve and whispered urgently in his ear.

"My client is, uh, not entirely aware of what voiceprints are."

Columbo glanced back and forth between the District Attorney and Grant Kellogg. "Well— We don't need to go into that right now. What I'm really wonderin' about, Miss Björling, is that anonymous call you got about Mr. Wylie murdering Miss Tammy Björling. Mr. Kellogg says that was in February. Is that right?"

Erika nodded. "January . . . February."

"An' it was in January or February that you, uh, wrote Mr. Wylie the note we found in the escritoire in his living room?"

She stared hard at him for a moment. "Yes . . ."

"But Mrs. Wylie says that's where they kept their postage stamps, so the note was not in that drawer all that time."

Glistening tears ran down Erika's red cheeks. "I don't know what he did with it, where he kept it. How could I know?"

"Uhhm . . . Kind of a mystery, isn't it? Lessee . . . Mr. Wylie gave you five thousand dollars in January. Was that before or after you sent him that note?"

"Before."

"Right. Or he might not have wanted to give you any more money. Right?"

"I suppose so."

Columbo shifted his eyes from Erika to Grant, to the District Attorney, then to Captain Sczciegel. "The way I understand, we gotta disclose any evidence we got. So— Miss Björling, do you know that ballpoint ink oxidizes?"

"What the hell is this?" Grant asked indignantly.

"I guess you didn't know," said Columbo. "And I guess Miss Björling didn't know either. But, y' see, the ink in a ballpoint pen is one chemical composition when it's up inside the tube in the cartridge; but when it's rolled out on paper, it dries, which means it oxidizes. It does that at a regular rate. A first-class chemical lab—which we got at LAPD—can analyze the ink on a sheet of paper and give a pretty good estimate of when that writing was written. Miss Björling, the note you wrote to Mr. Wylie was written within a few days before his death—a week at the most, maybe as little as two days."

Erika screamed and turned to Grant Kellogg and began to pound his arm and shoulder. *"You son of a bitch! You PROMISED me!"*

"Erika! Calm down! They got nothing—"

"Millions of fuckin' dollars! You and Sonya living on millions of fuckin' dollars, while I sit in the slammer doin' a *life sentence!* No *way,* you son of a bitch! *No way!"*

TWENTY-SIX

Friday, December 22

Adrienne was already at her table when Columbo walked into Emilio's. She had her usual martini in front of her and was wearing cream-white stirrup pants and a dark-blue cashmere sweater.

Columbo had checked his raincoat, and he had taken time to stop in the men's room and re-knot his necktie so the wide end hung below the narrow end.

"Sorry I'm late," he said. "Where's Dan?"

"He'll be *really* late. But he'll be here. Anyway, Merry Christmas and— Columbo! You're carrying a gun!"

"Yeah . . . " He looked down, saw that the Beretta was visible to anyone who looked, and quickly buttoned his jacket. "That's why I'm late. I had to go to the range and shoot this thing. Cap'n *ordered* me."

"Did you qualify?"

"Not exactly. But the range officer's a pal, and he'll send Captain Sczciegel a note sayin' I came awful close and will sure pass next time."

"How close *did* you come?"

Columbo grinned slyly. "I managed to make it shoot." He shook his head. "It's awful noisy, though."

The waiter who now came to their table was frowning and visibly disturbed.

"It's alright, José," Adrienne said. "This is Lieutenant Columbo, LAPD."

The waiter exhaled a relieved breath. "What can I bring you, Sir?"

"This bein' our Christmas lunch and all, maybe we ought to have a bottle of champagne."

"Sure. Absolutely. When Dan joins us. But have a Scotch first while I finish my martini."

"Yeah. Bring me a Glenfiddich on the rocks."

Adrienne smiled. "You're developing sophisticated tastes, Columbo."

"The man that introduced me to that kind of Scotch won't be drinkin' any for a while."

"Grant Kellogg?"

"Right. And, incidentally, thanks for the kind words."

He referred to her column published Tuesday—

CREDIT WHERE CREDIT IS DUE
DETECTIVE, NOT D.A., SANK KELLOGG
by Adrienne Boswell

Assistant District Attorney Charles Dunedin is to be commended for his aggressive and effective prosecution of Grant Kellogg, resulting in the life sentence imposed Monday. It should be noted, though, that he was able to achieve the conviction because of shrewd and dogged sleuthing done by a veteran detective lieutenant of the Los Angeles Police Department. Mr. Dunedin graciously acknowledges that it was Lieutenant Columbo who broke the case.

The Erika Björling testimony was, of course, the dramatic highlight of the trial. It was reinforced by the testimony of Sonya Pavlov and Fred Mansfield, who testified that Kellogg had offered them $100,000 apiece to perjure themselves to create an alibi for Miss Björling.

Although the testimony of those three witnesses sank the Kellogg defense, they were motivated to testify only because Detective Lieutenant Columbo had punched holes in the mercenary scheme concocted by Grant Kellogg. The detective had established, for example, that the notorious note threatening Tim Wylie had been written within days before the murder, not months earlier as Miss Björling and Mr. Kellogg had asserted. He had evidence also that voices recorded by Miss Björling's answering machine were the disguised voices of Mr. Kellogg and Miss Pavlov.

A dramatic break in the case occurred when Lieutenant Columbo produced evidence that Grant Kellogg was involved in an intimate affair with the principal alibi witness, Sonya Pavlov. Already made distraught by the damaging contradictions the detective had found in her story, Erika Björling became convinced that Kellogg was planning to let her go to prison while he and his new girlfriend enjoyed the profits from the murder she had committed at his behest. Faced with that, she broke down and accused her attorney of concocting the murder plot, telling her that Tim Wylie had murdered her daughter Tammy, and promising her not only revenge, but millions of dollars from the exploitation of her story.

Defense attorney Marvin Duke quotes Grant Kellogg as saying he knew he was in trouble when he learned that the chief investigator in the Wylie murder would be Lieutenant Columbo.

The detective says that Kellogg's overweening self-confidence did much to destroy him.

"Mrs. Columbo asked me to thank ya, too. She's been carrying the clipping around with her all week, and I don't think there's anybody left she hasn't shown it to."

"You're a modest man, Columbo, in a world that doesn't any longer count modesty as a virtue."

"I guess I'm an old-fashioned fellow, Adrienne."

She interrupted the conversation to allow the waiter to put his drink before him. Then she said, "You're old-fashioned enough to be able to feel sorry for people. I caught it that you feel sorry for Erika Björling."

He raised his glass in salute, then took a sip. "Y' got me."

"Let me tell you something that may make you feel a little better about her. I was with her yesterday. She's in the new women's prison, at Chowchilla. With squeaky-clean behavior and the sympathy most people feel, her ten-to-twenty is going to get her a parole in less than eight years. She's already done eight months. Hey! Eight months and eight days; she's got it exactly. So—"

"How *is* she?"

"She's miserable. What else? But she'll be fifty years old when she gets out, and she'll be a rich woman."

"How's *that* gonna happen?"

"What Grant Kellogg figured—only nothing for Grant Kellogg. I signed a contract last week for 'The Erika Björling Story.' Seven figures. She gets half."

"What about the law that says a criminal can't profit from books about—?"

Adrienne grinned and shook her head. " 'Son of Sam' laws. The Supreme Court of the United States knocked that notion into a cocked hat. When the book is out, we'll do a TV documentary on her. Seven more figures. Columbo—" Adrienne raised her glass. "Grant Kellogg's vicious plot is going to make two people *rich*. Erika . . . and *me!*"

"Everybody makes money off murder but me," said Columbo wryly.